Since 1988, national bestselling author **Rochelle Alers** has written more than eighty books and short stories. She has earned numerous honors, including the Zora Neale Hurston Award, the Vivian Stephens Award for Excellence in Romance Writing and a Career Achievement Award from *RT Book Reviews*. She is a member of Zeta Phi Beta Sorority, Inc., Iota Theta Zeta Chapter. A full-time writer, she lives in a charming hamlet on Long Island. Rochelle can be contacted through her website, www.rochellealers.org.

THE SHERIFF OF WICKHAM FALLS

ROCHELLE ALERS

MILLS & BOON

First Published in Great Britain 2018
by Mills & Boon, an imprint of HarperCollins*Publishers*
1 London Bridge Street, London, SE1 9GF

The Sheriff of Wickham Falls © 2018 Rochelle Alers

ISBN: 978-0-263-26529-3

0918

MIX
Paper from
responsible sources
FSC™ C007454

This book is produced from independently certified FSC™ paper to ensure responsible forest management.

For more information visit: www.harpercollins.co.uk/green

Printed and bound in Spain
by CPI, Barcelona

The Sheriff of Wickham Falls is dedicated to
my three brothers and late father—
all of whom honorably served in the US military.

Chapter One

Tap! Tap! Tap!

Natalia Hawkins opened one eye and then the other, and stared up at the ceiling in her bedroom; staccato tapping had jolted her out of her much-needed sleep, and she wasn't ready to accept that she'd moved into a house with a woodpecker living in a tree on the property.

Tap! Tap! Tap! Tap!

There it was again. After sitting up and sweeping off the sheet and lightweight blanket, Natalia swung her legs over the side of the bed. As soon as her bare feet touched the floor, she knew she would be up for the day. As a former ER doctor working in an over-crowded, understaffed Philadelphia municipal hospital, she was used to performing her duties on limited amounts of sleep.

She had believed Wickham Falls, a remote town in the Appalachian Mountains boasting a population of less than five thousand residents, was a place where she would no longer be jolted awake by honking horns from bumper-to-bumper rush hour traffic, the wailing of emergency vehicles' sirens or her name coming through the hospital's loudspeakers. She had left the noise of a large metropolitan city behind to get a peaceful night's sleep, only to be awakened by an annoying bird.

Natalia opened the blinds and bright early morning sunlight flooded the space. Her gaze lingered on boxes lined up against a wall that were filled with linens, blankets, clothes and shoes. There also were boxes in the smaller bedroom, the kitchen, bathroom, and living and dining rooms. It had taken less than six weeks for her to box up her life to leave behind all that was familiar to move and become a small-town family doctor—something she had always wanted, even before graduating medical school.

Slipping her feet into a pair of fluffy yellow SpongeBob slippers that were a Christmas gift from her eight-year-old niece, she walked out of the bedroom and into the bathroom. Although the compact one-story house was larger than her condo in the luxurious high-rise building in Philadelphia, it did not have the open floor plan or panoramic views to which Natalia had become accustomed. That no longer mattered because as soon as she opened the door to walk into the house, it became her sanctuary. She did not have to gird herself for a confrontation with her fiancé who had managed to find fault in everything. After a while, Natalia preferred sleeping at the hospital rather than come home to a hostile environment that had become even worse instead of getting better. And thanks to his duplicity, Daryl made it very easy for Natalia to make a clean break with her place of birth to follow and fulfill her dream to live and work in a small town.

She brushed her teeth and then washed her face as she stared at her reflection in the oval mirror over the pedestal sink. Even though she didn't look any different than she had in years, Natalia knew she wasn't the same woman who'd gotten her wish to become a doctor, and fall in love with a man she had thought of as perfect. She was still dedicated to her profession; however, her personal life had been filled with angst and turmoil. Her fiancé abruptly moved out of the condo four months ago, taking her engagement ring and the dog he'd given her as a gift for her birthday.

Natalia wasn't as upset about losing her ring as she had been about Daryl Owens taking Oreo, the dark-brown-and-white toy poodle that had been her constant companion. She'd promptly contacted the building's management to change the locks on the unit because she didn't want Daryl to return and renew what had become a toxic relationship where despite living under the same roof, they argued constantly and hadn't made love in months. The first night Natalia went to bed and woke up alone signaled a new beginning for her. And it took only a few days to realize she had been reborn and she didn't have to monitor every word or action because Daryl would invariably challenge and ridicule her.

Walking out of the bathroom, Natalia returned to the bedroom to make the bed. Normally she would head for the kitchen to brew a cup of coffee but that would have to be put off until she unpacked the coffee maker. She'd carefully planned her day to go into town for breakfast, and then stop at the hardware store to pick up paint, brushes and rollers to paint the kitchen. Shopping for groceries to stock the refrigerator and pantry was next on her to-do list, followed by unpacking as many boxes as she could to make her new home appear lived-in.

She fluffed up her pillows and positioned them against the wrought iron headboard, and had just opened the windows to let in fresh air when she heard a string of explosive expletives. Peering out the window, she saw a man holding his hand as he continued to spew curses, this time under his breath.

Instinct galvanized her into action as Natalia raced to the front door to see if the man had been seriously injured. She met a pair of light brown eyes in a face the color of golden-brown autumn leaves. He was tall, at least six inches above her five-five height, and powerfully built as evidenced by the white T-shirt stretched over a muscled chest and broad shoulders.

"Please, let me see your hand."

Seth Collier stared at the woman who seemingly had appeared out of nowhere. The pain in his left thumb intensified, throbbing as if it had its own heartbeat. "Who are you?" he asked her.

"I'm a doctor, and it appears as if you've injured your hand."

"You don't say," Seth drawled sarcastically. He'd accidently hit his thumb with the hammer when attempting to drive the last nail into the post for the birdhouse, fearing he had broken it. His gaze went from the face of the slightly built woman with a short natural hairstyle and a flawless complexion that looked like chocolate mousse to her chest. He had an unobstructed view of firm breasts in a floral tank top she had paired with red cotton lounging pajama pants. He averted his eyes before she caught him ogling her like a voyeur.

"Do you want me to look at your hand? There is a possibility that you have broken a bone."

Seth extended his hand at the same time he bit down on his lower lip; the pain had intensified. He couldn't remember the last time he'd injured himself while wielding a hammer. His general contractor father had taught him everything he needed to know about handling tools, but it was apparent he had temporarily forgotten the very important safety precautions. Seth blamed the accident on inattentiveness rather than fatigue. He'd left Savannah, Georgia, before midnight after spending a week with his mother and sisters, to drive back to Wickham Falls to arrive home at dawn. As soon as he pulled into his driveway, he saw the white BMW SUV parked next to the house that had been vacant for a year. His neighbor, who had planned to rent his house because he was out of the country, had asked him to watch his property. Not only was Seth surprised that someone had moved in, but as one of Wickham Falls' deputy sheriffs, there was very little that went on in the town that he wasn't aware of.

The second thing he noticed was the birdhouse he had put up once he'd moved back to The Falls was down again. Seth knew the boys who lived in the house on the street behind his tended to jump the fence rather than walk around the block, and in doing so knocked over the birdhouse. He had held off talking to their grandparents, who had taken in the boys while their parents were going through a contentious divorce, but now he knew he had to warn them about trespassing and vandalizing his property.

"Does that hurt?"

"No," he said, as the doctor massaged his fingers. It wasn't his hand but his thumb he'd injured, and thankfully he was right-handed or he wouldn't be able to perform his duties. Seth had another two days before he was scheduled to return to work.

"Try opening and closing your hand," she said in a quiet voice. Seth complied. "Lucky for you, you haven't broken any bones. I'm going to spray your thumb with a solution that will temporarily numb the pain. You hit your thumb rather hard, so you're going to experience some swelling. I recommend you apply ice several times a day to keep that down. Don't move. I'll be right back with the spray."

Despite the discomfort in his thumb, Seth found that he couldn't pull his gaze away from the sensual sway of her hips in the cotton pajama pants. He walked over to where she had parked her vehicle. The parking sticker from a Philadelphia medical center attached to the windshield with a caduceus verified she probably worked at a hospital. A hint of a smile touched the corners of his mouth. In that instant, having a medical professional as a neighbor was very convenient, otherwise he would have to wait for Dr. Henry Franklin to open his office or drive six miles to the county hospital.

The pretty physician returned, this time wearing

an oversize T-shirt with a faded University of Pennsylvania logo. So, he mused, she was an Ivy Leaguer, blessed with both beauty and brains. Seth hoped she hadn't noticed him staring at her breasts. He did not want her to believe she had moved next door to a pervert.

She sprayed his hand with an icy liquid, which miraculously alleviated the pain. "Now don't forget to ice it."

Seth flexed his thumb. Smiling, he said, "How much do I owe you?"

"Nothing, unless you wake me up again before seven in the morning with that annoying hammering."

Seth managed to look contrite. "I'm sorry about that. The kids who live on Woodfield Road hopped my fence and knocked over the birdhouse. I was attempting to repair it."

"You could've waited until later in the day to repair it," she admonished in a quiet voice.

He stared at her back as she turned and walked away. "What's your name, miss?" he called out.

She stopped, but did not turn around. "Dr. Hawkins."

"Thank you, Dr. Hawkins." When she didn't acknowledge his offer of gratitude as she entered her house, he muttered "you're welcome" under his breath.

Things usually moved at a snail's pace in The Falls, but it was apparent it had only taken less than two weeks for him to get a new neighbor. And when Natalia identified herself as a doctor, Seth wondered if she was going to take over Dr. Franklin's practice or join the staff at the county hospital.

After walking back to his driveway, he picked up

the birdhouse and rested it against the side of the house. He wanted to delay putting it up again until he spoke to the grandparents of the teenage boys who used his backyard as a shortcut. Recalling Dr. Hawkins's recommendation that he apply ice to his thumb, Seth opened the side door and went inside to follow her instructions.

Natalia parked the SUV in front of the hardware store. Downtown Wickham Falls reminded her of many of the bucolic East coast towns that were settled when the States were still British colonies. Vehicles were parked diagonally to maximize space along the four-block-long business district. Both sides of the three blocks were lined with mom-and-pop shops, a local bank, a supermarket, the post office, the fire department and government buildings that included the town hall, courthouse, sheriff's department and jail. Dr. Franklin's medical office was a one-story building flanked by a law office and a barbershop.

During her first trip to Wickham Falls in early March when she interviewed with Dr. Franklin, she had noticed there were no chain drugstores, big-box warehouses or fast-food restaurants. Not having easy access to delicatessens or coffee shops had her second-guessing whether she wanted to relocate to a town where she would have to get into her car and drive miles to find the nearest strip mall. It was only after contacting a local realtor and touring the town that Natalia was able to appreciate its quaint charm. It no longer mattered that railroad tracks dissected Main Street, or that there were only two stoplights: one in front of the fire department, and another near the school campus.

The woman had shown her two vacant homes that were up for sale, but Natalia knew she wasn't ready to purchase a house, and then she asked if there were any that she could rent perhaps with the option to buy after a year. And within minutes of walking into the one-story, refurbished, furnished home with stark-white walls and updated appliances, she knew it would suit her needs. The owner had secured a two-year post teaching English at a Japanese university and had decided to rent the house in lieu of selling it. He'd been gone a year, which now allowed Natalia the next twelve months to decide on a permanent residence.

It was nine o'clock and the business district was waking up. Shopkeepers were sweeping and then hosing down sidewalks in front of their businesses. Natalia realized it would take her a while to get used to a lifestyle that seemed to move much slower than she was used to. She'd had to drive to a restaurant off the interstate for breakfast, because Ruthie's, the local eating establishment, did not open to the public until eleven.

She walked into Grand Hardware and saw a man who looked like a department store Santa Claus without the red suit. His bright blue eyes sparkled like polished blue topaz when he smiled.

"Good morning, ma'am. How can I help you this morning?"

Natalia returned his friendly smile with one of her own. "I need two gallons of high-quality latex, semi-gloss paint, several brushes and some rollers with extension poles, a pan and liners, tape and drop cloths."

The rotund middle-aged man with snow-white hair and a matching mustache and beard patted his belly over a bibbed apron. "What color are you looking for?"

The kitchen was a stark-white, a shade she found much too sterile. "Let me see your paint samples." It took her less than five minutes to select a color labeled Harbor Mist. It was a pale blue-gray, a shade that would complement the stainless-steel appliances and bleached pine cabinetry. "Do have paint that can cover stains?"

"That means you need one with a primer. It will eliminate you applying more than one coat."

Forty minutes after walking into the hardware store, Natalia had selected everything she needed to give the kitchen a new coat of paint, while Johnnie Lee Grand talked nonstop about the preparations for the town's upcoming Memorial Day parade until he left her to wait on another customer.

She loaded her purchases in the cargo area of her SUV, and then drove down the street to the supermarket. An hour later, the shopping cart was nearly overflowing with items to stock the pantry and the refrigerator-freezer. Natalia generously tipped the young man who bagged and stacked the bags neatly in her vehicle. She was more than impressed with the selection of fresh meat and poultry in the butcher department. She could not remember the last time she would have structured her work hours where she would be able to come home and prepare dinner for herself. Natalia rarely ate fast food, and the hospital's cafeteria menu, although deemed nutritious, rarely varied from day to day.

The downtown area was bustling with activity when she left the supermarket and headed back to the house. It was May 1, and while winter was just loosening it brutal grip on Philadelphia, spring was in full bloom in southeastern West Virginia. The daytime temperature was in the low seventies, trees had put forth their leaves as did flowering plants their colorful yield. The cacophony of bird chatter as they flitted from branch to branch had become music to Natalia's ears.

I think I'm really going to like living in Wickham Falls, she mused as she maneuvered into the driveway to the house on Stewart Avenue. Most of the homes along the street sat on one-square-acre parcels that were larger than those in other areas of the town. And of all of the houses on the avenue, the one she occupied was the smallest.

She'd just exited the SUV when she saw her neighbor sitting on his porch. "How's the thumb?"

He rose and leaned over the porch railing. "It's still swollen, so I'm taking your advice and icing it."

Natalia smiled. "That's good."

"Do you need help unloading your car?"

She shook her head. "No, thank you."

"I think you do," he countered when she set several bags on the ground.

"I'm really good here." Her protestations were ignored when he came down off the porch and stood next to her.

"Why don't you go and open the door and I'll bring everything in?"

Natalia tilted her head and stared up at the man with balanced features and large golden-brown laughing eyes. Stubble on his strong, square jaw enhanced his overt virility. She had viewed more naked men than she could count since entering medical school, yet there was something about her neighbor's physique that reminded her of the perfection of the male human body. And it was obvious he worked out because she couldn't detect an ounce of fat on his torso under the white T-shirt.

"It's all right, Mr.—"

"Collier," he said, interrupting her. "The name is Seth Collier. And yours? Because as neighbors I shouldn't have to refer to you as Dr. Hawkins."

"It's Natalia. I can take the bags. I don't want you to reinjure your thumb."

Seth smiled, exhibiting perfectly aligned white teeth. "And if I do, then you can tend to me again."

Natalia returned his smile. "If I treat you again, then I'll have to send you a bill."

"That's okay because I do have medical insurance. Now, please go and unlock your door so I can bring in your groceries." He peered in one of the bags. "You need to put your perishables in the fridge before they go bad."

"Okay."

She walked up the porch to her house and unlocked the screen door, and then the inner door. Seth had brought in four bags, setting them on the floor in the living room, when she walked past him to bring in more.

"What are you painting?" he asked when he placed the paint cans next to the bag with the brushes and rollers.

"The kitchen."

Seth crossed muscular arms over his chest. "Who's going to do the painting?"

"I am." Natalia picked up the bags with the dairy products and headed for the kitchen.

Seth followed, carrying two bags in each hand. "That's not a small job."

She smiled at him over her shoulder. "I know. It should take me a couple of days before I finish. I didn't have to buy a ladder because I found one in the utility closet near the back door."

"You could finish a lot sooner if I help you."

Natalia gave Seth a lingering stare. She did not find him off-putting or even threatening, but she wasn't used to strangers offering their services within hours of her meeting them. "Don't you have a job, Mr. Collier?"

"It's Seth, and yes, I have a job. Right now I'm on vacation, so I'm trying to be neighborly and also appreciative for you treating my hand. If you hadn't, then I would've had to wait for Dr. Franklin to open his office before he could see me, or drive six miles to the county hospital and spend half the morning in the ER. You're new to The Falls, and I want to let you know that folks here always help out their neighbors."

She nodded. "You're right. I am new here, so it's going to take a while before I get used to your way of doing things. And how can I repay you if I allow you to help me?"

A hint of a smile tilted the corners of Seth's firm mouth. "I'd like a home-cooked meal."

A laugh slipped through Natalia's parted lips. "You want me to cook for you?" Seth nodded. "How do you know if I can put together a palatable meal?"

His eyebrows lifted a fraction. "You didn't buy

all of this fresh food just to look at it. Otherwise you would've selected prepackaged meals."

"What about your wife or your girlfriend, Seth? Do they cook for you?"

"No, because I don't have a wife or a girlfriend. My cooking skills are passable, and when I don't cook for myself, then I'll occasionally eat at Ruthie's or the Wolf Den. I'm certain you passed Ruthie's on your way to the supermarket, while the Wolf Den is a sports bar located between here and Mineral Springs."

Natalia began emptying the bag with milk, butter, eggs, yogurt and cheese. She could not begin to imagine why a man who looked like Seth wasn't married or involved with a woman.

"What exactly do you do when you're not on vacation?"

"I'm a deputy."

She blinked slowly. "You're a US deputy marshal?"

"No. I'm Wickham Falls' deputy sheriff. And what brings you to The Falls?"

Natalia opened the French door refrigerator and then moved several open boxes of baking soda to the back before she stored the perishables on shelves and in drawers. "I'm here to assist Dr. Franklin."

Seth applauded. "Well, it's about time he hired someone to help him out. Folks have been known to spend hours in his office waiting for him to see them just for a follow-up visit."

"That's because he's very thorough," Natalia said in defense of her new boss. She'd watched him examine one of his patients who had come in complaining of back pain.

"Thorough and very, very slow," Seth countered. "When do you want to start painting?" he asked.

"Today," she confirmed.

"If we work together I'm certain we can finish today."

Natalia wanted to tell Seth that she still had to un- pack boxes, but didn't want to appear ungrateful. "If I'm going to spend the entire afternoon painting, then I can't cook for you."

"That's not a problem. I'll take you to the Wolf Den tonight and you can cook for me tomorrow."

Natalia did not want to believe her neighbor had mentioned taking her out to eat as if it was something they'd done before. And she hoped he didn't think of it as a date, because she wasn't ready to date any man, even one as attractive as her next-door neighbor. "You're really on this kick for me to cook for you."

"I told you it's been a while since I've had a decent home-cooked meal."

Despite his obvious arrogance, Natalia did not want to believe she had hit the jackpot when it came to a neighbor. Not only was he tall, dark and deli- ciously handsome, but he was also willing to donate his time to help her paint. "Do you usually moonlight as a painter in your spare time?"

Throwing back his head, Seth laughed loudly. "Not quite. My dad was a local handyman." He held up his left hand when Natalia opened her mouth. "Don't say it," he warned softly.

"Don't say what?" she said as she struggled not to smile.

"You were going to mention my hitting my hand instead of the nail."

"That's called an accident," she said, rather than tease him about his mishap with the hammer. "Give me about twenty minutes to put everything away and for me to change my clothes, and then we can begin painting. I'll leave the door unlocked for you."

Her eyes met Seth's. The magnetism coming off him in waves held her captive until Natalia dropped her gaze. She could feel pinpoints of heat stinging her face and she was grateful for her darker complexion to conceal what would've been an obvious blush. And she also prayed he hadn't caught her staring at him like a starstruck groupie coming face-to-face with her idol.

Seth gave her a mock salute. "I'll see you later."

Natalia exhaled an audible breath of relief when Seth walked out of the kitchen. She had relocated to Wickham Falls to become a small-town doctor, and had no intention of falling under the spell of her sexy neighbor.

Chapter Two

Seth wasn't certain why he had volunteered to help Natalia paint the kitchen because he knew her treating his hand had little to do with it. However, he did appreciate her concern, which told him she hadn't hesitated when she believed he'd seriously injured himself. And he had been truthful when he told her that folks living in Wickham Falls looked out for one another.

He'd spent the first eighteen years of his life in The Falls and the next eighteen serving his country as a marine. Now, at thirty-eight, he was back to stay. Unlike some kids who couldn't wait to grow up to leave, it had been different with Seth. Perhaps it had something to do with reconnecting with his parents and sisters, because each time he was granted leave it was to come back to his hometown.

He walked into his house and descended the staircase to the basement. In the two years since his honorable discharge, Seth spent most of his spare time working on the house where he had grown up. He had updated the kitchen and finished the basement. He'd also had a company put on a new roof and replace worn shingles with vinyl siding.

Seth knew he had disappointed his late father when after graduating high school he refused to join Adam Collier's general contracting business. But, the elder Collier understood his son's wish to embark on a military career because of the stories he'd told Seth about serving in Vietnam, as well as Seth's grandfather fighting in Korea.

Seth opened the door to a storeroom and selected an extension pole for a paint roller, a pan and several pan liners, a pair of safety glasses and a package of respirators to prevent the inhaling of paint fumes. He checked the shelves and made a mental note to restock several items the next time he went to Grand Hardware. Like most residents in The Falls, Seth made a concerted effort to shop locally, although he could save a lot more money by shopping in the stores off the interstate.

Ten years ago, members on the town council embarked on a shop locally campaign to sustain the viability of the independent stores in the business district. Every couple of years, they voted down proposals to allow national chains or franchises in Wickham Falls, much to the delight of local business owners.

Gathering what he needed for the painting project, Seth returned to the first story. The throbbing in his left thumb was an indication he had to ice it again.

He retrieved an ice pack from the freezer and placed it over his hand. He'd hoped the swelling would disappear before he was scheduled to return to work. The sheriff, an ex-marine drill sergeant, who was noticeably out of shape himself, expected all of his deputies to be physically and mentally fit to perform their duties.

After icing his thumb, Seth exchanged his jeans and T-shirt for a pair of painter bib overalls, a long-sleeved cotton polo and paint-spattered running shoes, then covered his head with a tattered baseball cap. He felt as comfortable in what he deemed work clothes as he had in his military police and deputy sheriff uniform.

Natalia had emptied the bags and stored her groceries in the refrigerator-freezer, on shelves in the miniscule pantry, and had changed out of her blouse and jeans and into a pair of shorts she should've discarded last summer and an oversize white T-shirt. A pair of flip-flops had replaced the ballet flats. She debated whether to cover her short hair with a hat or a bandanna, and then decided on the latter.

Affecting a short, natural wash-and-go hairstyle had been advantageous when working double, and on occasion triple, shifts at the hospital. Then she would shower in the doctors' lounge, grab at least four hours of sleep, then go back on duty. She had been so sleep-deprived, Natalia knew she would never catch up on the hours she'd lost. She was looking forward to assisting Dr. Franklin, because not only would it be a different environment but she would be able to develop a relationship with her patients.

Natalia left the bedroom and walked into the kitchen, smiling when she saw Seth standing on the ladder and putting blue tape around the windows, cabinets and along the ceiling. He'd removed the stools at the breakfast island and covered the countertops and the round oaken table and four chairs in the eat-in kitchen with drop cloths. The radio positioned under a row of overhead cabinets was tuned to a station playing soft jazz.

"I didn't hear you come in," she said. Seth had entered the house so quietly that Natalia hadn't detected his presence.

Seth glanced at her over his shoulder. "That's a warning that you should keep at least one of the doors locked whenever you're home alone, because you don't want someone to walk in on you. Nowadays you have to take every precaution to protect yourself."

"Wickham Falls is so small that I thought there wouldn't be a lot of crime here."

He climbed down off of the ladder. "We don't have much when compared to larger towns or cities but there is crime here."

"What about opiates?" Natalia asked.

Turning slowly, he gave her a direct stare. "Did Dr. Franklin tell you about our drug problem?"

Natalia shook her head. "He didn't have to. It's become an epidemic that's affecting large and small cities and towns throughout the country. Even the so-called affluent neighborhoods aren't exempt."

"Amen," Seth confirmed under his breath. He opened a gallon of paint, attached the pour spout and slowly drizzled paint from the can into the pan with a liner, then repeated the action with the second one.

"I brought over an extra pan for the paint, so we can both use rollers."

Natalia glanced around the kitchen. "How long do you think it's going to take us to finish painting this?"

"Probably about two to three hours."

"What I don't understand is the walls in the other rooms are spotless, while the kitchen is a mess."

The house's pristine condition and updated appliances, along with a washer and dryer in the unfinished basement, were the reasons Natalia had decided to rent it. When she'd questioned the realtor why the home had remained vacant for a year, the woman said interested tenants complained that the rent, which included a two-month security fee, was out of their price range, but for Natalia it was less than what she'd once paid for her mortgage and maintenance on her condo.

"I'm willing to bet that Chandler's nephews are the culprits," Seth said.

"Mrs. Riley at the realty company told me that my absentee landlord is a confirmed bachelor and lived alone."

"He is and does, but every once in a while, his sister would drop off her twin boys and that's when chaos erupted. Chandler and his sister were raised by a single mother. They were never allowed to have friends over because Mrs. Evans said she didn't want them tracking dirt inside. Chandler is also a neat freak, but he's also a very indulgent uncle when it comes to his nephews."

Although she was curious to know more about her landlord *and* her neighbor, Natalia decided not to question Seth further because she wanted them to finish their painting project. Picking up a disposable respirator, she put it on and then protected her hands with a pair of rubber gloves.

Natalia stood next to Seth admiring their handi-work. They'd completed painting the kitchen in less than two hours. The bluish-gray color was the perfect complement for the stainless-steel appliances. "You did a very nice job, Seth."

Attractive lines fanned out around his eyes when he smiled. "So did you," he countered. "And I'm will-ing to bet that this isn't your first painting project."

Folding her arms under her breasts, Natalia nod-ded. "The year I turned thirteen, I asked my mother if I could paint my bedroom and she said okay as long as it wasn't black. One year it was fluorescent pink, and another year it was lavender. I was in the pink and purple phase for a while until I left for col-lege. It was only after I graduated medical school that Mom told me since I was a doctor, I'd forfeited the room and she was going to paint it with a color of her choice. My mother liked oyster-white walls, which I've always found much too sterile. Although Mom tells everyone she's a very modern woman in reality, she's very conservative."

"There's something to be said for conservatism."

Natalia glanced up at Seth. "You're a conserva-tive?"

He angled his head. "I'm more of a traditionalist middle-of-the-road guy."

"Is that another way of saying you're old-school?"

"Not as much old-school as I am a conventional person. Give me the rules and tell me the law and I will follow them without question."

"So, if you were to stop me for speeding, I'd never be able to talk you out of giving me a citation even if I told you I was going to a medical emergency."

"That would be the exception because if it's a 911 call, I'd escort you to see your patient."

Natalia knew without question that Seth was inflexible when it came to bending the rules, and she wondered if it was the reason why he wasn't married or had a girlfriend. That it was his way or the highway.

"Well, let's hope I don't have too many medical emergencies," she said in a quiet voice.

"Are you going to alternate hours with Dr. Franklin?" Seth asked.

"Not initially. We'll work together for a couple of months until we're able to establish a routine where we may be able to have at least two late nights to see patients. Speaking of patients, let me look at your thumb again."

"It's okay."

"It can't be okay if you're massaging it," Natalia said accusingly.

Seth let go of his left hand. He hadn't realized he was manipulating his thumb to ease some of the tightness in the digit. Some of the swelling had gone down, but now it appeared to have stiffened. "I hit it pretty hard so it's going to take a few days before I stop favoring it."

Natalia reached for his hand, cradling it in her much smaller one. "Do you want me to spray it again?"

He snatched his hand away. "No! I'll ice it again when I get home."

"You can apply a warm compress after you ice it again."

Seth smiled. "I'll do that. I'm going to clean up here—"

"Please don't," Natalia, said, cutting him off. "You've done enough. I'll clean up everything. And dinner tonight is my treat."

Seth shook his head. "No, it's not. I never allow a woman to pick up the check when we go out together."

"I'm not your date, Seth."

"Whether you are or are not my date is irrelevant. I still won't let you pay for my meal."

"What if we go dutch?"

Not wishing to engage in a verbal confrontation, something he'd done much too often with some women in his past, he forced a smile that did not reach his eyes. "It's almost three o'clock now, and I'd like to pick you up at six. Is that too early?"

"Oh… I mean no. It's not too early."

"If that's the case, then I'll see you later."

Turning on his heel, Seth walked out of the kitchen. It had been less than twelve hours since he met his new neighbor, and there was something about her that intrigued him. He was more than curious about the woman driving a top-of-the-line luxury SUV bearing Pennsylvania plates, and why she was renting a house in The Falls. Seth knew he could easily find out more about his new neighbor by entering her vehicle's license plate number into a national database accessible to law enforcement but that would be the same as snooping. After all, she wasn't a suspect or a person of interest in a case he was investigating. And he hoped, after sharing a meal with Natalia, she would answer some of the questions that had him wondering why she had come to The Falls.

Natalia dipped the sable brush into the compact with loose powder that was specially blended to match her complexion, and tapped it lightly against the lid to shake off the surplus before she drew it over her face. Peering into the mirror over the bathroom sink, she stared at her handiwork. Although it had been a while since she'd applied foundation, eye shadow, mascara and lipstick, it was apparent she hadn't lost her touch. A moisturizer and occasionally lip gloss were the only allowances she made for makeup when working at the hospital, and the last time she made up her face was New Year's Eve when she'd accompanied her ex to a party hosted by one of the partners at his law firm.

What had begun as a festive evening ended with them glaring at each other after Daryl accused her of flirting with one of his colleagues. The incident foreshadowed the end of what had become a fragile relationship when she vowed never to attend another social soiree with him unless he apologized for his rude behavior. She waited weeks, and then a month, for him to express regret, but when he didn't Natalia knew it was time to end their engagement. However, Daryl beat her to it when he moved out and took off with her ring and her dog.

Now she was preparing to go out with her neighbor. The major difference was that it wasn't what Natalia deemed a traditional date. However, she had admit to herself that she did find Seth Collier very, very attractive, but even that wasn't enough for her to think of him as anything other than someone who lived next door. She found it ironic that she'd lived in the condo for eight years and had never socialized with any of the other residents in her building. Although they would occasionally greet one another with a nod or perfunctory greeting, she didn't know any of their names. Picking up a wide-tooth comb, she ran it through the strands of her short hair and then using her fingers, fluffed them to achieve greater height. Preparing to resign from her position at the hospital, closing on the sale of the condo to her sister and brother-in-law, and then packing the personal items she planned to ship to Wickham Falls hadn't left time for her to visit her favorite Philly salon for a trim. Fortunately, time was no longer an issue for Natalia with her working shorter hours and she had to decide whether to let her hair grow out or keep it short and virtually maintenance-free.

The ring of the doorbell startled her as she hurriedly washed her hands and left the bathroom to answer the door. The clock on the living room fireplace mantelpiece chimed the hour. It was exactly six o'clock. Seth said he would pick her up at six and arriving at the appointed time revealed he was a man of his word.

She unlocked the inner door to find Seth standing on the porch staring at her with an expression she interpreted as temporary shock. She unlatched the storm door and held it open. He'd changed into black slacks with a white untucked shirt open at the neck and spit-shined black boots. Much to her disappointment the stubble from his lean, strong jaw was missing. Natalia wasn't a big fan of facial hair, but somehow she liked it on Seth.

"Please, come in. I just have to get my jacket and purse."

"That's all right. I'll wait here for you."

Seth had told Natalia he would wait on the porch for her because it would give him time to recover from staring at her slender body in a pair of body-hugging black stretch slacks, high-heeled booties and a black-and-white striped silk blouse.

When Natalia opened the door, Seth felt as if someone had hit him in the chest, causing him to lose his breath, when he stared at her. He couldn't believe the transformation. She'd gone from a fresh-faced ingenue to a seductress with smoky eye shadow and a raspberry mouth that made him want to taste her lush lips to see if they were as sweet as they appeared. It had been a while since he'd slept with a woman, but that still did not explain his reaction to a woman who unknowingly had him wanting to spend time with her.

And there were a few questions he wanted her to answer for him: why had she chosen to practice medicine in Wickham Falls and not some other town? Who or what was the reason for her leaving a cosmopolitan city like Philadelphia to live in a town where more than half the populous were at or below the poverty line, and at the same time census numbers were steadily decreasing?

A smile parted his lips when she returned wearing a loose-fitting black peplum jacket. Her big-city sophistication was definitely on display, and he wondered how long it would take for her to conform to a more relaxed style of dress. Jeans, boots or running shoes were the norm for most residents. Even the local church had eased dress code restrictions where women attended services in slacks, and some of the teenage girls had attempted to push the envelope when they showed up in shorts and tank tops.

The scent of Natalia's perfume wafted to his nostrils when she closed and then locked the doors. "You look very nice," Seth complimented.

Natalia's demurely lowered her eyes. "Thank you."

Cradling her elbow, he led her down off the porch and over to his driveway where he'd parked the Dodge Charger. Seth opened the passenger-side door and waited until Natalia was seated and belted in before he rounded the car to sit behind the wheel. He didn't get to drive the powerful muscle car as often as he liked. He had driven it to Savannah and back, but most times he drove his late father's Ram Pickup to and from the station house to keep it from sitting too long. Even though the sixteen-year-old vehicle had more than a hundred thousand miles on the odometer it still handled like new. His father had claimed the great loves in his life were his wife and children, and then his pickup, which he worked on tirelessly to keep it in tip-top condition.

"How far is the Wolf Den from here?" Natalia asked when they stopped at the railroad crossing. The gates were down, bells were ringing and red lights were flashing indicating an oncoming train.

Seth shifted into Park, and then stared at Natalia's delicate profile as she looked out the windshield. "It's on the edge of town between The Falls and Mineral Springs."

She turned to meet his eyes. "Why isn't it located downtown like the other businesses?"

"During Prohibition, the Gibson brothers decided they'd had enough of being miners and pooled their meager savings to buy some land off the beaten track to set up a still to sell moonshine. And to stay one step ahead of the revenuers they built the restaurant as a front for their illegal activities."

"Were they ever caught and prosecuted?"

Seth smiled. "No. There was no way folks were going to snitch on them because it would cut off their supply of some of the best hooch in the county. Once Prohibition was repealed, the Gibsons wanted to move the restaurant into town, but several town council members retaliated and passed a law prohibiting the sale of alcohol within the business district. They'd assumed it was their way of punishing them for breaking the law, but it backfired. The Den became even more popular among those folks because they had a place where they could drink openly and eat some of the best barbecue food in Johnson County."

"What about Ruthie's?"

"Ruthie's is a family style, all-you-can-eat buffet restaurant. Their busiest times are weekends when kids are out of school and also when families gather there following church services."

A slight frown furrowed Natalia's smooth forehead. "Are you saying Sunday dinners are passé?"

"It is with some families."

"When I grew up we had a tradition that the first Sunday in each month the extended family would get together. We'd rotate homes. One Sunday it would be our house, and then it would be one of my aunts. My grandmothers would compete with each other as to who could come up with the best desserts. Most times it was a draw because whatever they made was spectacular."

Seth chuckled. "Everyone brags about their grandmother's cooking. You'll discover that during our Fourth of July bake-off competition. Around here, holidays are cause for the entire town to turn out and celebrate. We have the upcoming Memorial Day parade and picnic."

"Mr. Grand at the hardware store was bending my ear about the parade," Natalia said, smiling.

"It's a big deal in The Falls because of so many active military and former veterans."

"Like you?"

Seth nodded. "Yes, like me. I suppose you noticed the American and US Marine Corps flags attached to the porch."

"That and the Semper Fidelis decal on the bumper of this car," she said, laughing softly. "Is it true once a marine, always a marine?"

"Yes, ma'am."

"What other holidays do you celebrate big-time?"

"The Fourth of July. We combine that with three nights of carnival rides, games and food contests. Labor Day is a little low-key with family cookouts. Then the whole town also turns out to celebrate Halloween. There are games and a photo gallery where parents can pose in costume with their children. After sunset, there are tailgate parties, hayrides and bonfires with folks taking turns reading ghost stories. It's the perfect segue to our Fall Frolic, Thanksgiving and then Christmas. Once most of the mines closed and kids were leaving to join the military or find employment elsewhere, those who couldn't or didn't want to leave The Falls look forward to the town-wide get-togethers."

"It must have been fun growing up here with all of the holiday celebrations."

"It was and still is," Seth confirmed. "The adults have as much fun as their children."

Natalia stared at the passing cars of the freight train, some of them carrying hazardous materials, and remembered the excitement in Johnnie Lee Grand's voice when he talked nonstop about the upcoming parade and wondered if Seth would become a participant.

"How many people leave and come back?" she asked.

She realized she was asking way too many questions, but it served as a foil not to think about the man sitting inches from her. There was something about Seth that made it impossible for her to ignore him. She found his overall virility, soothing drawling voice and smiling light brown eyes fascinating.

Resting an arm over the back of her seat, Seth exhaled an audible sigh. "Not too many. There was a time when my father was drafted to serve in Vietnam that most of the boys who survived came back to work in the mines like their fathers, grandfathers and generations of men before them. Then after the mines closed, most of those who went into the military didn't bother to come back because there were no jobs for them. The members of the town council have repeatedly voted down allowing chains to set up here because although it would provide employment opportunities, the downside is it would also put local shopkeepers out of business."

Natalia turned slightly to give Seth a long, penetrating stare. "What made your dad come back?"

"A pretty girl who was in college studying to become a schoolteacher caught his eye. My father had just begun dating my mother when his number came up. He wanted to marry her before being shipped out, but she refused, saying she didn't want to be a young war widow. She told him if and when he came back she would marry him. He made it through the war physically unscathed except for occasional flashbacks which plagued him for years. He married my mother and because he was good at fixing things, he started up a home repair business. Dad could glance at a diagram of something and put it together without looking at it again."

"So, your father was never a coal miner?"

"No. But my grandfather and his father before him were. Grandpa used to say all of us were different colors when we went down in the mines, but at the end of the day when we came out, we were all the same color from the coal dust."

"And it was the same when they were diagnosed with black lung," Natalia whispered.

"You're right about that. Mining was both a blessing and a curse. It provided men with money to take care of their wives and children, but it also destroyed entire families when fathers, grandfathers, sons, brothers and uncles were killed or injured because of unsafe conditions. If you travel throughout the state you'll see memorials erected to honor those who lost their lives in mine disasters."

Natalia remembered television coverage of a mining disaster in West Virginia when she was in her last year of medical school. Experts reported it was preventable because the owners had neglected to install safety systems. The mines may have closed in and around Wickham Falls, but mining for coal, copper, silver, iron, lead, diamonds, gemstones and other minerals was still in operation in the States and all over the world.

"Why did you come back?"

"Initially I'd planned to make the military my career, but after eighteen years, I came back to be with my mother after my father passed away. My father had retired and my sisters who were living in Georgia were begging them to move closer to their grandchildren. Mom would've gone years ago, but Dad didn't want to leave his buddies who got together every week to play cards and trade war stories. Four months after I became a civilian, the sheriff approached me to join the department as a deputy because he knew I'd been military police. Once I was sworn in, Mom told me she was moving to Savannah, so I utilized my GI bill and bought the house from her. She moved into a townhome several blocks from my younger sister."

Natalia smiled. "So, you're one of the rare ones who left and came back to stay."

The last car of the freight train clattered past as Seth put the car in gear and drove over the tracks. "It wasn't something I'd planned until I was much older, but even the best made plans can go awry."

"I hear you," she said under her breath.

When she'd accepted Daryl's marriage proposal, Natalia felt as if all of the pieces of her life were falling into place. She'd realized her dream to become a doctor, and had met and fallen in love with a brilliant litigator who'd landed a position with one of Philadelphia's most prestigious law firms. He had pursued her relentlessly for two years until she'd agreed to become his wife, but then he changed much like a snake shedding his skin when he went from easygoing to someone she didn't recognized. She'd made allowances for the shift in his behavior to the added responsibility of becoming partner, but once his controlling and ongoing criticisms about her appearance impacted her emotional well-being, Natalia decided she'd had enough and began pushing back. Disagreements escalated into shouting matches after which they wouldn't speak to each other for days. Physical intimacy declined and then stopped altogether when Daryl spent more time in his condo than he did in hers. They continued to attend social events as a couple unbeknownst to others that their relationship was as fragile as eggshells.

"How long do you intend to work here before you return to Pennsylvania?"

Seth's query shattered Natalia's reverie. "I won't know until the end of next April."

He gave her sidelong glance. "What's happening then?"

"That's when I'll let Dr. Franklin know if I intend to join his practice as a partner."

"And if you don't?"

"Then I'll have to decide where I want to go. It'll probably be in another small town because I've had enough of municipal hospitals with staff shortages, shrinking budgets and endless bureaucratic red tape.

I've always wanted to be a small-town doctor and living and working here will give me the experience I'll need to establish my own practice."

"Let's hope you'll find a permanent home here because we need you."

Chapter Three

Seth escorted Natalia into the Wolf Den, his hand resting at the small of her back. He felt her go stiff against his palm before she went pliant. When he'd told her that *we* need you, he had included himself in that equation. He didn't want her as a girlfriend but as a friend. It had been a few years since he could count a woman among his friends.

The conversations among those seated at the bar stopped when customers spotted him with Natalia. The locals were used to seeing him come in wearing his uniform, but rarely in street clothes or with a woman. He nodded and exchanged greetings with those with whom he had reconnected since returning to The Falls. Transitioning to life as a civilian had gone smoothly for Seth, which he attributed to frequent trips home. He didn't know what it was, but there was something about his hometown that drew him back again and again. Even when his mother announced that she was moving to Savannah, Seth had the option of reenlisting or becoming a federal agent with the Marine Corps Criminal Investigation Division. He had taken advantage of his GI education benefit to obtain a bachelor's in criminal justice and had six remaining credits to complete to obtain a graduate degree in the same field.

He had been truthful with Natalia when he told her he'd wanted to return to live in Wickham Falls, but only after he retired from the military and law enforcement. If he'd served in the corps for twenty years and another twenty as a federal agent he would be fifty-eight, still young enough to enjoy fishing, traveling and tinkering around his house. Not once had the notion of having his own family figured into his future plans once his divorce was finalized.

Seth had known when he married Melissa, life would be challenging for his young wife. She had complained that she felt like a nomad packing up their apartment and moving whenever he received orders to transfer to a different base. The final straw came when he was deployed to Afghanistan. When he returned to the States, it was to discover his wife was carrying another man's child. Her excuse that she was lonely and he wasn't there for her fell on deaf ears. Seth filed for divorce, ending their three-year marriage, and then signed up for his second deployment.

"Hey, Seth, where have you been hiding yourself?" the bartender shouted.

One of the regulars, a retired postal worker sitting at the bar, raised his mug of beer. "Fletcher's right.

Me and the boys were talking about not seeing you around. We thought you had re-upped."

Smiling, Seth patted the older man's back. "It's called a vacation, Jesse."

"Good for you and good for us. Sheriff Jensen would be up the creek if he lost you." The others sitting at the bar echoed his sentiment. "By the way, who's your pretty girlfriend?"

Seth stared at Natalia when she glanced up at him. He was suddenly aware that being seen with her would generate some gossip. He lowered his head. "Do you want to introduce yourself?" he said in her ear.

Natalia knew it was only a matter of time before all of Wickham Falls would know who she was, not as Seth's girlfriend but as Dr. Franklin's assistant. "I'm Natalia Hawkins, and Seth and I are just friends," she added, smiling.

"If that's the case, I'm available if you're looking for a boyfriend," called out a man with a shaved pate, a full strawberry blonde beard and both arms covered with colorful tattoos.

Natalia laughed along with the others. "I just got rid of a boyfriend so I'm really not looking for another one right about now," she said truthfully.

Seth's arm curved around her waist. "Let's find a booth before someone puts a ring on your finger."

Natalia wanted to tell him someone had put a ring on her finger, and if she could turn back the clock she never would've accepted it. "Do women who come here always get propositioned?" she asked Seth.

He waited for her to slip into the booth before sitting opposite her. "I've never witnessed it before. I'm glad you took it all in stride because they're really harmless."

She smiled, and then lowered her eyes. "I wasn't insulted." Natalia wanted to tell Seth that she'd found it flattering that men would flirt with her because it had been much too long since she'd thought of herself as pretty. Wearing scrubs and no makeup had become the norm for her rather than the exception. Even when she'd dressed up for Daryl's firm's New Year's Eve party, what she'd felt inside was reflected in her demeanor when she refused to smile and join in the festivities. It was then she realized no amount of makeup or haute couture could mask the instability of a doomed relationship that was evident by her expression, and now knew moving to Wickham Falls was one of the best decisions she had made in her life, thus far.

The people she'd met were friendly, unpretentious and weren't afraid to speak their minds. She'd experienced countless catcalls from men who felt it was their right to say whatever came to their mind, but something communicated to Natalia that the men in the Wolf Den were different. She was certain if she had revealed she was Seth's girlfriend, then the flirting would've ended immediately.

"Now that they know you're not my girlfriend, news is going to spread like a wildfire that you're available," Seth said in a quiet voice.

Her eyes met his. "Whether I'm dating anyone or not is not a problem for me because I'm not looking to get into a relationship."

"Is it true you just got rid of a boyfriend?"

She paused for several seconds, and then said, "He wasn't a boyfriend but a fiancé."

"What happened to…" Seth's words trailed off when a middle-aged waitress with fire-engine red hair came over and placed two menus on the table.

"Hey, handsome," she crooned, winking at Seth. "I missed seeing you last week."

Seth smiled at the woman who'd recently switched with her daughter from the lunch to dinner shift. "I took some time off to visit my mother and sisters."

"By the way how is your mom?" the waitress asked as she set napkins and place settings on the table.

"She's well, Sharleen. Thanks for asking."

"Please send her my regards." She paused. "Where are your manners, Seth? Aren't you going to introduce me to your lady friend? Or should I've said your girlfriend?"

Seth wondered how many more times he and Natalia would have to deny they were romantically linked; since he'd returned to live in Wickham Falls no one had seen him with a woman. "Natalia, this is Sharleen Weaver. Sharleen, Natalia Hawkins," he said introducing the women and deliberately ignoring the waitress's reference to Natalia being his girlfriend.

Sharleen rested her hands at her waist. "It's nice meeting you, Natalia. Will we get to see you again?"

"I'm sure you will," Natalia replied.

"Is there anything I can bring you good folks to drink before you order?" Sharleen asked.

Seth angled his head and stared at Natalia. "Do you want anything from the bar?"

"No, thank you. I'll just have water."

Sharleen nodded. "Seth, should I bring you your usual?"

"Please, Sharleen." Leaning against the back of the booth, Seth waited until Sharleen left before focusing his attention on Natalia. She'd mentioned a fiancé and he wondered who'd initiated the breakup. "I'm sorry folks think we're a couple."

A slight smile played at the corners of her mouth. "It's not about me as much as it is about you, Seth," she countered.

"Why would you say that?"

"You claim you don't have a girlfriend or a wife, so it's apparent when people see you with a woman they assume she must be special enough for you to be seen in public with her. And it doesn't bother me what they say or think because we're neighbors and nothing more."

Seth knew Natalia was right about them being neighbors. "That's something we both can agree on." A beat passed before he asked, "How did you get the name Natalia?"

"My mother taught college-level romance languages and literature, and had decided if she had children they would all have Latin names. I'm Natalia, which means 'nativity' because her due date with me was December 25. My sister is Serena, but everyone calls her Rena, and my brother is Justin."

"Should I assume Justin implies justice?"

"Not so much justice as just or upright."

Seth rested his forearms on the table. "Were you born on Christmas Day?"

"No," Natalia said, smiling. "I came two days earlier but still close enough to Christmas for Mom to keep the name."

"Where are you in the birth order?"

"I'm the middle child. And before you ask, I never went through the middle child syndrome. My parents treated all of us the same. But if you listen to my pompous brother, he'd tell that he's their favorite because he's the firstborn *and* male."

Nodding slowly, Seth flashed a Cheshire cat grin and winked at Natalia. "I think I like your brother."

"Please don't tell me you're older than your sisters."

His grin became a wide smile. "Bingo. I was responsible for protecting my sisters and carrying on the Collier name."

"Do you have a son or sons?"

"No, but—"

"But nothing," Natalia said, cutting him off. "If you don't have a son, then you can't say you're carrying on the Collier name."

"That's not to say it won't happen one of these days."

"When you're fifty?" she teased.

Seth narrowed his eyes. "So the doctor has jokes."

Natalia's expression mirrored innocence. "No. Either you're forty or close to it, and you profess not to be married or have a girlfriend all which translates into either you're commitment-shy or you plan to become a baby daddy."

"You're wrong on both counts. I'm not afraid of committing because I was married once. And I have no intention of ever becoming a baby daddy." He saw Natalia's face crumble like an accordion and wondered if she was comparing her failed engagement with his unsuccessful marriage.

"I'm sorry if I prejudged you," she whispered.

Seth flashed a smile. "There's no need to apologize. Some things just don't work out the way we'd like."

"How true," Natalia remarked.

"Is he the reason you moved here?" The query was out before Seth could censor himself. He'd just met Natalia and he didn't want to turn her off by prying into her love life.

She averted her eyes. "He wasn't the only reason, but I'd rather not talk about that now. I haven't eaten since this morning, and I'm ready to order everything on the menu."

Seth laughed under his breath. "So, you're not one of those women who eat like a bird because they're monitoring everything that goes into their mouth?"

Natalia rolled her eyes upward. "That's sexist, Seth. There are men who also are just as finicky when it comes to their diets. And do I look anorexic to you?"

Seth knew he'd put his proverbial foot in his mouth and had to be careful taking it out. "Um…no. I'm sorry I mentioned it."

"How much weight I gain or lose has never been a concern of mine. There were occasions when I worked eighteen hours in the ER that I'd take time out to drink a smoothie or grab a salad because it saved time. But whenever I had several days off I'd make all of my favorite dishes and sit down like a normal person to enjoy my meals."

"I suppose all of that will change now that you'll be working with Dr. Franklin."

* * *

Natalia nodded. Her entire life had changed since leaving Philadelphia. "Yes, it will." She opened the menu binder and perused the selections. "What do you recommend?"

Seth pointed to the chalkboard on the opposite wall. "Everything's good, but I usually order the day's special."

She glanced at the board. "I'm going to order the smothered chicken with steamed cabbage and rice." Natalia paused. "How's the white bean soup with ham?"

He smiled. "It's excellent. You must have been reading my mind because I was going to start out with a cup."

Natalia closed the binder. "I'm also going to have one."

Sharleen returned with her water and Seth's club soda, and took their dining selections. Minutes later, she came back with their soup. The mouthwatering aroma wafting from the cup was a blatant reminder of how long it had been since Natalia had eaten breakfast.

She took a spoonful and closed her eyes. When she opened them she found Seth smiling at her. "You're right. It is delicious."

"Everything they make here is incredible and that's why the Den has managed to survive after so many years when restaurants in other towns have gone out of business."

"Good food and the fact that there are no fast-food restaurants around here," Natalia said once she swallowed another mouthful of the soup made with navy beans and pieces of smoked ham.

"Fast food notwithstanding, if the Den didn't offer palatable dishes it wouldn't have survived."

"What about Ruthie's?" Natalia asked.

Seth picked up his spoon. "Ruthie's is good if you're looking for variety. And because what they offer is not processed and prepared daily, it is much healthier than fast food. Another good thing is the owners of Ruthie's and the Den donate all leftovers to our soup kitchen."

"There's a soup kitchen here in Wickham Falls?"

"Yes. It's a part of the church's outreach."

Seth gave Natalia a steady stare. "Poor farming techniques and the loss of jobs to mechanization in the mining industry have led to out-migration, and coupled with that, Appalachia has always had a problem with tax revenue and absentee land ownership has left many counties with hard-core pockets of poverty."

She lowered her eyes. "I suppose I'm going to have to study up on the history of my new state."

"You may not have to study too hard because I'm willing to bet your patients will give you an earful. Everyone has a tale to tell about their grandmother or grandpappy."

Natalia finished her soup and laced her fingers together on the Formica tabletop. "How was it for you growing up here?"

Seth closed his eyes as a dreamy expression flitted over his features. "It was great. I didn't realize we were poor because there was always food on the table and a roof over our heads."

Sharleen set their orders on the table and over din-

ner, Natalia listened to Seth talk about three generations of Collier men working in the mines until his
father was forced to choose another vocation once the
mines began closing down. She pretended interest in
the food on her plate because each time she glanced
up, she found Seth staring at her.

"Dad's number came up in the draft several months
after he graduated high school. Once he returned to
The Falls, he hired himself out as a handyman, extending credit to those unable to pay in full. Folks
called on him to repair a leaky roof, busted pipes
and rewire their home. Even though we had a little
more than many other families my mother drummed
it into our heads that we were no better than those who
bought their food with government-issued stamps, or
kids that wore hand-me-downs.

"I started going with Dad to his jobs once I entered
high school. He wanted me to work with him after I
graduated, while my mother insisted I go to college.
It was the only time I witnessed my parents arguing
with each other. I decided to enlist and have the military pay for my college education. I managed to give
both my parents what they wanted when I earned a
degree in criminal justice and whenever I came home
on leave I'd spend that time helping Dad."

Natalia took a sip of water. "That sounds like a
win-win for everyone."

Seth nodded. "Yes, it was. Enough talk about me
and my family. Have your brother or sister made you
an auntie?"

"My brother has. He and his wife became parents
for the second time last year. My sister just celebrated
her second wedding anniversary a couple of months

ago, and she and her husband have decided to wait a few years before they start a family."

"Are you one of those aunties that spoil their nieces or nephews?"

"I will when they're old enough. My nieces are still too young for them to help me bake cookies or have sleepovers."

"Speaking of cooking, what do you plan to make tomorrow?"

"Look at you," Natalia teased, smiling. "You just ate and you're already talking about more food."

"What can I say? I like to eat. However, I do work out to stay in shape for my job."

Natalia wanted to tell Seth that during her second trip to Wickham Falls to secure housing she saw a deputy with a conspicuous potbelly that indicated he wasn't as physically fit as he could've been. "Where do you work out?"

"I've set up space in the basement to use as an in-home gym. You're welcome to come and use it whenever you have time."

"Thanks for the offer, but I packed my bike along with some other things I wanted to bring with me." Daryl had turned her on to biking and she had taken to it like a duck to water. "Riding a bike around here is going to test my stamina because of the hills."

"We have the Appalachian and Allegheny Mountains running through the state, so you won't find too many places where the land is flat. What else do you do for relaxation?"

A wry smile touched her mouth. "That's about it."

Resting an elbow on the table, Seth cradled his chin on his fist. "Have you ever gone fly-fishing?"

"No, but it's something I'd like to do." She'd gone fishing with her Scout group but never caught anything.

"Maybe one of these days I'll take you fishing with me."

Natalia felt a shiver of excitement eddy through her. Now that she wouldn't be required to work around the clock, she would have time to do some of the things she'd dreamed about doing. She'd always been an outdoorsy person from the time she'd joined the Girl Scouts. Hiking, canoeing, sleeping outdoors in a tent and roasting marshmallows over a campfire were the highlights of her childhood.

"I'd love that. You have to let me know where I can buy some equipment."

"You don't have to buy anything. I have all of the fishing tackle we'll need. I'll even bait your hook for you."

"Do you really think I'd be afraid of a worm when I've treated people with injuries where their entrails were hanging out of their bodies?"

Seth put up both hands. "My bad!"

"Outwardly I may appear to be a city girl, but underneath all of this" she pantomimed running her hand over her body "I'm a country girl at heart."

"Where does your country come from?"

"Attending medical school in the South made me aware of my Southern roots. My grandfather was born and raised in DC. He attended Howard University and then their medical school. Once he became a doctor he moved to Philly and set up a practice. He married his nurse and together they had four boys—all of whom became doctors."

With wide eyes, Seth stared at Natalia. "Are your siblings also doctors?"

"No," Natalia said, laughing. "Justin is an urban planner for the city of Philadelphia and Rena an underwriter for an international insurance company."

"Where did you attend medical school?"

"Meharry College School of Medicine in Nashville, Tennessee."

Seth's eyebrows lifted slightly. "Why didn't you go to Howard like your grandfather?"

"Once I realized Meharry is the first medical school in the South for African Americans and also the oldest and largest historically black academic health science institution, I knew it's where I wanted to go. Did you know that less than five percent of the doctors in this country are black?"

"No, I didn't. Those numbers are pathetic."

"That was one of the reasons I wanted to be a doctor and to become a role model for little girls who look like me. I used to watch the faces of young women I'd treated and they would light up once I told them I was Dr. Hawkins and that I was going to try and make them feel better. Some even questioned whether I was really a doctor and I had to convince them that I was."

"Can I say that Philly's loss is The Falls' gain?"

"Hopefully you're right about that." Natalia knew working in a private practice would be a dramatic change from the ongoing chaos in a large city hospital's emergency room. She doubted whether she would have to treat a number of gunshots and knifings, but that did not exempt her from medical crises stemming from household accidents or responding to drug overdoses. Seth had confirmed what Dr. Franklin had told her about the increase of abuse of opiates in the town.

The noise in the restaurant escalated appreciably when several couples walked in. "I think it's time we leave to free up the table unless you'd like dessert," Seth said.

"No, I'm good." And she was. Not only had Natalia enjoyed the food but also her dining partner. Seth was a refreshing change from going out with Daryl who felt it was his divine right to select the restaurant because he had an expense account while also attempting to order for her, and whenever she refused he'd spend the time sulking like a spoiled little boy.

It was only after their breakup that she'd questioned herself as to why she had stayed in their relationship so long. She'd convinced herself she was in love and attributed the ongoing tension between them to the stress in their careers. It had taken less than twenty-four hours to conclude after Daryl walked out that she had been liberated from a prison without bars.

Seth settled the bill and then escorted her out to the parking lot packed with vehicles. It was Friday and date night. Natalia stared at the sky and inhaled a lungful of cool, crisp mountain air. How different, she mused, nightfall in the mountains was from the city. The sun had slipped behind the mountains leaving streaks of orange and bloodred color across the darkening sky.

"Spectacular, isn't it?" Seth whispered in Natalia's ear as he moved closer to open the passenger-side door for her.

The heat coming from his body, his moist breath caressing her cheek and the seductive scent of Seth's cologne wrapped Natalia in a comforting cocoon from which she did not want to escape. "Yes, it is," she whispered.

Seth took a step back and she slipped into the car. "Do you want to go for a drive before I take you home?"

Natalia glanced up at him. "Perhaps another time. I still have some unpacking to do, and I also have to figure out what I want to cook tomorrow."

The seconds ticked as he stared at her. "Forget about cooking for me. It was selfish of me to put that pressure on you when you're trying to settle in. Please let me finish, Natalia," he said in a quiet voice when she opened her mouth. "We're going to be neighbors for the next year and hopefully I'll get a chance to sample your home cooking at least once during that time."

Her smile successfully concealed her disappointment because she was looking forward to spending more time with Seth. She'd felt more comfortable with him than she had with any other man in years. Nothing in his demeanor indicated he was trying to come on to her which had put her completely at ease.

She suspected, after she'd mentioned she'd had an ex-fiancé, that he probably wanted to know what had happened but did not pry for which she was grateful. Talking about Daryl always put her in a funk that left her in a bad mood for days. Natalia didn't blame her ex as much as she did herself. She had free will and the option of continuing to see him or end their toxic relationship. However, she had deluded herself when she said it would get better, that he would change. But instead of getting better it got worse and worse until she knew it had reached a point where it had to be resolved. Days before he walked out, Natalia had confided in her sister that she was going to break up with Daryl before Valentine's Day. Rena applauded her position while admitting she never liked her fiancé because he was full of himself. Thankfully Daryl's leaving made the break drama-free, because when it came to drama, her ex could take it to another level.

Natalia buckled her seat belt when Seth slipped in behind the wheel. They exchanged a glance and smile before he started the engine and backed out of the parking space. She had no way of knowing when she rented the little house on Stewart Avenue that she would live next door to a gorgeous, hunky lawman.

There was only the humming sound of the car's powerful engine during the drive back home. Natalia wanted to remind Seth that he was exceeding the town's speed limit but held her tongue when she realized the chances of him being pulled over for speeding were nonexistent because he represented law enforcement.

"You were speeding," she said when he opened the door to assist her. She placed her hand in his and he eased her to a stand.

"So you noticed?"

"Shame on you, Seth. You took an oath to uphold the law and meanwhile you just broke it."

Tightening his hold on her hand, Seth led her across the lawn and up to the porch. He lowered his head, and dropped a kiss on her hair. "Good night, Natalia. Now go inside and lock the door behind you."

The porch lights had come on and provided enough illumination for her to see him trying not to laugh.

"Good night, Seth." She unlocked the door, entered the house and locked it behind her.

Resting her back against the door, Natalia closed her eyes and slowly let out her breath. Her first twenty-four hours in Wickham Falls had just become a little more interesting. Not only did people recognize one another on sight but they also appeared privy to their personal lives. Seth was greeted by other diners who appeared genuinely surprised to find him dining with a woman. He'd admitted that he had been married and Natalia wondered if she had also been a local girl.

She shook her head as if banishing all thoughts of Seth. When she told him she wasn't looking to get into another relationship, it was a reminder to her and a subtle warning to him that they could never be more to each other than friends and neighbors.

Natalia removed her makeup, and then changed into a pair of sweatpants and a T-shirt before she tackled the task of opening boxes and putting things away. It was close to midnight when she finally crawled into bed and fell asleep within minutes of her head touching the pillow. She did not wake again until ribbons of sunlight slipped through the slats of the blinds.

Chapter Four

Seth woke feeling more tired than he had when going to bed. He'd slept fitfully. For the past two nights, images of Natalia's face appeared in his dreams and he knew he hadn't been honest with himself. He'd convinced himself that he wanted them to be friends when in reality he wanted them to be more.

There were questions he wanted to ask Natalia about the man she had been engaged to but decided to wait until she felt comfortable enough to talk about her past.

He'd found Natalia easy to be with and talk to. What impressed him was her modesty. She had to have had above average intelligence to become a medical doctor. Even her reason for choosing a historically black medical school rather than one affiliated with an Ivy League college resonated with him. She had not forgotten where her ancestors had come from, who she was and the impact she could have on young women looking for a career in the medical profession.

Seth flexed his left thumb. Most of the swelling had gone down and there was only slight discomfort in the digit. He had decided to wait another day before he put up the birdhouse, but first he had to talk to the grandparents of the young boys responsible for jumping the fence protecting his property from theirs. Tossing back the sheet and lightweight blanket covering his nude body, he swung his legs over the side of the bed and headed for the bathroom to prepare for his first day back to work.

Seth walked around the corner and found Mr. and Mrs. Crawford sitting on the porch in matching rockers. He stopped halfway up the steps and forced a smile he didn't feel. "Good afternoon, Mr. Crawford."

Howard Crawford nodded. The network of tiny lines crisscrossing his face was the result of decades of working outdoors repairing roads for the county. "Good afternoon, son. What brings you here?"

Seth registered the older man's defensive tone and decided not to say anything that would end in a verbal confrontation. "I'd like to talk to you about your grandsons jumping my fence and knocking over the birdhouse."

"When did this happen?" Mrs. Crawford asked.

He smiled at the woman who was the epitome of a grandmother with her white hair and friendly blue eyes. "It was one day last week when I was out of town."

"If you weren't here, then what makes you so certain it was my grandsons?" Harold asked, his voice rising slightly.

"I have cameras on my property, and when I viewed the footage I saw the boys climbing over the fence."

Seth had installed the cameras to deter break-ins and keep intruders from stealing his firearms. And when at home he always secured his service and off-duty automatic handguns in a safe in the bedroom closet.

"What can I say, Seth, but boys will be boys," Harold said glibly.

Seth closed his eyes for several seconds to compose himself. "I intend to say this once, Mr. Crawford. If your grandsons jump my fence again, I'm going to arrest them for trespassing and vandalism, and then you'll have to answer to the local judge about them being just boys."

Harold sat straight as a noticeable flush swept over his features. "You wouldn't."

"Yes, I would. I came here hoping we could resolve this without threats, but if you think I'm just blowing smoke then try me. Keep your boys off my property." Seth wanted to frighten the man into talking to his grandchildren about respecting someone's property. If left unchecked, they could possibly grow into adults with little or no regard for the law.

Seth must have gotten through to the older man when he nodded. "I'm sorry, Deputy. I'll talk to them."

Mrs. Crawford rounded on her husband. "Don't just talk to them, Harold. You have to put the fear of God into those boys or they'll end up like their daddy who can't stay out of trouble even if you offered him a million dollars."

"You know they won't listen to me," Harold countered. "Deputy, can you do me a favor and talk to them?"

Seth detested getting drawn into domestic squabbles but knew this time it was necessary because it directly concerned him. "Okay."

He waited while Harold went inside to get his grandsons. Ten minutes later they emerged still wearing pajamas although it was early Sunday afternoon. Although they weren't twins, the two boys were mirror images of each other. Both claimed coal-black hair, large hazel eyes and a sprinkling of freckles over their noses. Seth estimated they were between ten and twelve, impressionable ages when young boys could either take the right or wrong path in life.

"Jason and Mikey, Deputy Collier wants to talk to you boys about trespassing on his property," Harold said, glaring at his grandsons.

Seth saw fear in the eyes of the brothers as they stared up at him and he rested a hand on each of their shoulders. "I wanted to talk to you guys about climbing over my fence and knocking over the birdhouse."

The younger boy sniffled and wiped his nose with the back of his hand. "We go over the fence because it is a shortcut to the school bus."

"You can no longer use my yard as a shortcut. When you come onto someone's property without their permission it's called trespassing. Do you know what that means?" The brothers nodded.

"Am I...are we in trouble?" Jason, the older brother asked.

"Not this time." Seth smiled when they blew out breaths at the same time. "But you will be if you knock over my birdhouse again."

"We won't go over the fence again," Mikey promised.

"And we won't go in your yard," Jason added, "because Grandpa said we are going back to Florida to live with Mama once school is out."

Seth hoped the boys' parents had worked out an amicable divorce. He remembered their mother as a popular, outgoing girl with a penchant for dating and eventually marrying an alleged bad boy from Kentucky. He extended his hand. "Now that we understand one another, let's shake on it." He shook Mikey's hand and then Jason's before they raced up the porch and went back into the house.

Harold approached Seth. "Thank you. You handled that nicely."

"I didn't want to come down too heavily on them but hopefully they got the message."

"Trust me, they did. It hasn't been easy for them with their momma and daddy fighting all the time. But thankfully it's over now that Kaitlyn's been granted full custody."

"Divorce is always hard, Mr. Crawford, especially when children are involved."

Fortunately for Seth, when he divorced his wife, children hadn't figured into the equation—at least not his child. When he'd returned to the States he was met with the news that his wife was pregnant with another man's baby. She'd asked for a divorce so she could marry her lover before the birth of their child. Seth made it easy for her when they flew to the Dominican

Republic, filed and were granted a quickie divorce. He'd acknowledged some blame for the breakup of his marriage on being away from home for extended periods of time, yet he'd felt if Melissa wanted out, then she should've communicated that to him.

The older man grunted. "That bum never wanted his kids. He's always made my girl's life a living hell." He offered Seth his hand. "Thank you again. I'll definitely let Kaitlyn know you talked to her boys."

Seth shook the proffered hand. "No problem." And it wasn't a problem whenever he diffused a situation with a conversation rather than physical force or an arrest.

"Are you marching in the Memorial Day parade?" Harold asked.

"It all depends on my schedule, but I'll certainly be there. I'd like to stay and chat but I have to go to work."

"Be careful out there, Deputy."

Seth smiled and waved as he turned on his heel and walked around the corner to his house. His vacation was over and now it was time to fulfill his oath to protect and serve the residents of Wickham Falls. His steps slowed when he saw Natalia sitting on her porch reading.

"How's it going, Natalia?"

Natalia's head popped up. "It's all good. I'm going inside in a few minutes to begin cooking, and if you have time you're more than welcome to join me."

He rested a foot on the first step. "I would if I didn't have to go to work. My shift begins at two and I'm not off until ten tonight."

Pushing off the rocker, she came to her feet. "Is that your regular hours?"

Seth stared at her bare face silently admiring the flawlessness of her brown complexion. To say Natalia was a natural beauty was an understatement. He had always preferred women who were comfortable in their own skin.

"Yes, it is." There had been a time before his hire where the deputies had worked twelve straight hours.

"How many days do you get off each week?"

He angled his head, wondering what she was hatching in her beautiful head. "Two. Why?"

"I was trying to figure out when we'd go fishing. I still have to work out my schedule with Dr. Franklin before you and I can get together."

"You're really serious about fishing, aren't you?"

Natalia took a step and rested a hip against the porch column. "Yes, I am," she said, smiling. "I was reading up on recreation in the region and fishing, hunting, hiking and white-water rafting were at the top of the list. I don't hunt and I've never gone rafting but I am open to fishing and hiking."

"You'll need a fishing license. You can apply for one at the town hall who'll file it with the Johnson County clerk. It'll take about a week before you'll get the license in the mail and it will it be valid until the end of the year."

Natalia nodded. "I'll definitely apply for one."

"I'd love to stay and chat, but I have to change." It was the beginning of May and that meant he didn't have to wear the fall and winter regulation wool-blend gray uniform with a matching wide-brimmed felt hat.

He preferred lightweight khaki and the dark brown straw hat even during the winter months.

"Stay safe."

Smiling, Seth nodded. "Thanks. I will." Seth gave her mock salute. "See you around."

Natalia returned his salute. "See you around," she repeated.

Seth parked the pickup in his assigned spot at the rear of the sheriff's office. It felt strange to return to work after being off for two weeks. In the past, he'd taken his fifteen-day accrued vacation time a week at a time. Swiping his ID card, he waited for the light to change from red to green and then pushed open the door. The sheriff's office and jail were connected with a passageway to the courthouse to minimize attention during the transfer of a prisoner from lockup to the courtroom. Most of the crimes in The Falls were misdemeanors that were quickly adjudicated by the local judge. Those charged with a felony were incarcerated until the judge signed off for them to be picked up by Johnson County law enforcement personnel.

The sheriff was in his office, feet propped on the corner of the desk, as he talked on the phone. Seth waved to him as he made his way over to his desk where he found a pile of folders. Before leaving for vacation he had cleared up all of his pending paperwork. He smothered a curse under his breath, and knew without a doubt the cases belonged to assistant deputy sheriff Andy Thomas. Andy had become the assistant deputy because of longevity, not skill or dedication. Although he was extremely popular with the residents Andy had been warned about his dereliction of duty, and Seth knew Sheriff Jensen would've fired Andy if he'd been able to replace him.

There had been a time when the town had the sheriff and two deputies, which on occasion left the department shorthanded. However, when Roger Jensen had become aware of Seth's return to Wickham Falls, he'd offered him the position. Roger went to the members of the town council and asked them to authorize the hire of an additional deputy. The fact that Seth was a native son coupled with his military police experience had the members fast-tracking the approval and the mayor swore Seth in as the town's newest deputy.

"What's all of this, Georgina?" he asked the long-time day clerk who'd just come back from her break.

Georgina Reeves had practically grown up in the position. Her father, who'd been sheriff before Roger was elected to the position, hired her directly out of high school to oversee the office. There was a lot of talk about nepotism although there was no regulation in the books that would prohibit family members from working in the same department. She was responsible for answering phones, fielding complaints and clerical work. There was a running joke among the townspeople that Georgina never married or had children because she was wedded to her job.

She rolled her eyes upward. "Those are Andy's end-of-the-month cases. He's been out with back pain for the past three days. Roger wants you to review his reports to make certain his stats are accurate."

Seth slowly shook his head. "Did he go to the doctor?"

Georgina made a sucking sound with her tongue and teeth. "Please, Seth, don't start me lying. For the life of me I don't know why Roger won't give him the boot because he's always complaining about either his legs or his back."

Seth smiled at the attractive middle-aged woman as Georgina patted the salt-and-pepper chignon on the nape of her long neck. With her dark hair and violet-hued eyes she'd earned the sobriquet of Wickham Falls' Elizabeth Taylor. "The military calls it goldbricking."

"And I call it being lazy," Georgina spat out.

Seth knew talking about Andy would only delay getting the files completed before Georgina entered the statistics into the town's database. He booted up the computer on his desk and pulled up the file on those who had been processed through their department. Infractions usually ranged from speeding tickets to disorderly conduct, domestic disturbances and possession with the intent to sell. He usually began with completing paperwork, and then went out on patrol. He scheduled his dinner break at six, continued patrols until the business district closed down, and then returned to the station house to await the deputy to relieve him.

He'd just finished reviewing Andy's arrest reports when Roger came over to sit on the swivel chair next to his desk. The springs groaned as if in pain when the sheriff settled into a more comfortable position.

"I need a chair that doesn't cry whenever someone sits in it," Seth remarked.

"Someone who isn't carrying more weight than they need to," Roger said under his breath. He ran a hand over his thinning gray hair. "Mrs. Jensen has been nagging me to either go on a diet or work out but we both know that's not going to happen until I retire, and that's not going to be for a while."

Seth stared at the man who'd been the town's sheriff for more than thirty years. When first elected, Roger was at least fifty pounds lighter and claimed a full head of dark brown hair. He'd just celebrated his sixty-second birthday and judging from his perpetually florid complexion and labored breathing, Seth prayed the man would survive to seventy—the mandatory retirement age for municipal employees.

"I've told you before that you're welcome to come to my place and use my workout equipment."

Roger laced his fingers together over his belly. "I'll probably take you up on your offer but only after I check with Dr. Franklin. The last time I saw him he told me not to begin an exercise program until I've had a complete physical."

"Just let me know when you're ready. This is just a suggestion, but I think you should send a requisition to the town council for new office equipment," Seth said when the chair creaked again, the sound resembling nails on a chalkboard. "We don't need someone suing us when they fall off that chair." The year before the council members had allocated funds to purchase new computer and telephone equipment, and to replace a police cruiser that had been totaled when it slipped off the road and crashed into a tree during an ice storm.

Roger nodded. "I'll have Georgina pull up the budget to see if we have enough to buy a couple of chairs."

"I've finished checking Andy's files, so I'm going to head out now."

"I'm sorry that you had to go over Andy's files."

Roger's brow lowered in a frown. "I'd fire him like yesterday if I could find another deputy to replace him. I've asked around and posted the position but so far no takers. And I prefer someone with former military experience."

Seth successfully hid his shock behind an impassive expression. It was the first time he'd heard Roger talk about firing Andy who continually shirked his duties. He wasn't certain whether the assistant deputy had been on the job so long that he'd become complacent. Seth had also noticed since his hire that the sheriff had also mellowed, becoming more laid-back and tolerant.

"Who have you asked?"

"Giles Wainwright."

Seth slumped lower in the chair. The year before, Giles Wainwright had married a local girl who lived in the house opposite his on Stewart Avenue. They'd bonded immediately because both had served in the Corps and had long conversations about their prior military service. Giles occasionally asked Seth to keep an eye on his house whenever he took his wife and daughter with him when they traveled to New York and the Bahamas to manage his family's overseas real estate holdings.

"What did he say?"

"He was very gracious and thanked me for asking and said once he left the military, he didn't want to pick up a firearm again."

Seth wanted to tell Roger that talking to Andy wasn't going to solve his problem of supervising his assistant. After a verbal warning, then he would have to follow that up with a written reprimand, which would give him the documentation he'd need to fire the deputy. But as the newest hire and not a supervisor Seth decided to keep his advice to himself.

Roger stretched out his legs at the same time the worn chair springs groaned under his bulk. "Can you do me a favor?"

Seth eyed him with skepticism. When Roger asked for a favor it usually meant working extra hours. Even if he was compensated with accruing comp time or pay, Seth had begun to jealously guard his personal time. "What do you need?"

"I need to go up to Charleston tomorrow for a few days to take care of some family business and I want you to take over for me while I'm away. If Andy wasn't out with his back problems I would've asked him."

"Have you cleared this with Andy?" Seth didn't want to usurp the assistant deputy's responsibility in the chain of command.

"I just spoke to him. Of course he wanted to come back, but I told him not until he gets a doctor's note clearing him to return to duty. I also sent an email to the mayor apprising him of everything."

Roger wanting him to run the department until his return meant Seth's work schedule would begin at six in the morning and end twelve hours later. "Okay."

The sheriff exhaled an audible sigh. "Thanks, Seth. You can go home now and rest up before you come in tomorrow morning."

"What about Connor?"

"He'll be here in a couple of hours. Now that his wife is pregnant again he can use the overtime."

Seth would've preferred Roger giving him this information before coming into the station house, but he wasn't going to look the proverbial gift horse in the mouth now that he'd been granted an additional day off.

Natalia filled a large pot with water and set it on the stovetop. She had debated whether to bake a chicken or make a pasta dish with sausage, and the latter won out. She had gotten the recipe from her medical school roommate who in turn had inherited it from her Italian restauranteur uncles. And Natalia had Adrienne to thank for many of the recipes that had been passed down through generations of Caputos. Adrienne had taught her to make fresh pasta for ravioli, crepes for manicotti, marinara sauce from San Marzano tomatoes and bread from scratch.

She'd just lowered the flame under the pot when the doorbell chimed, the sound startling her. Natalia wiped her hands on a towel as she walked out of the kitchen to answer the bell. Peering through the sidelight, she saw Seth standing on the porch and unlocked the inner door, and then the outer one, her smile matching his when he held up a bottle of red and a bottle of white wine in either hand.

"Am I too early or too late for dinner?"

Natalia noticed he wasn't wearing his uniform; he had on a pair of black jeans with an untucked ice-blue banded collar shirt. "I thought you had to go to work."

"The boss changed my hours."

She opened the door wider. "Please come in. You're just in time."

Seth wiped his booted feet on the thick straw rug

and walked into the house. He lifted his head and sniffed the air. "Something smells good."

"I'm baking focaccia."

"I didn't know the supermarket sold frozen focaccia bread."

"I didn't buy it," Natalia admitted.

His eyebrows lifted. "You make your own bread?"

Turning on her heel, Natalia headed back to the kitchen. "Yes, but only when I have the time." She glanced at him over her shoulder. "I hope you like Italian food."

Seth smiled. "I like food."

Natalia laughed. "And I like to cook. I always make too much, so if you're not too proud to accept handouts, then let me know if you're willing to accept an extra portion."

Cooking, reading, listening to music and viewing her favorite movies had become her escape from the ongoing frenetic chaos in a big-city hospital's underfunded and understaffed emergency room. She was never able to make plans to join friends or family members for a social gathering because she hadn't known if she would be able to meet them at the predetermined time.

"I accept but it must go both ways."

She stopped and met his eyes. "You're going to cook for me?"

He set the wine bottles on the countertop. "Why not? I'm no gourmet chef, but thanks to my grandmother's recipes I can put a palatable meal on the table."

Natalia winked at Seth. "So, grandmamma taught her grandbaby boy how to cook," she teased.

Seth slowly shook his head. "No. She taught my mother, who in turn had inherited Grammie's recipes. Even though Mom gave me the notebook I've rarely used it."

Natalia, curious as to what Seth would prepare, extended her hand. "You've got yourself a deal."

He shook her hand. "Deal it is."

She returned to the stove and removed the top from the Dutch oven. The aroma from fennel, onion, garlic and crumbled sweet sausage in a sauce made with dry white wine, heavy cream, half-and-half and tomato paste filled the kitchen.

"It looks as if I really have to step up my game," Seth drawled as he peered over Natalia's shoulder. "That looks and smells delicious."

A slight shiver eddied over Natalia when the heat from his body and the sensual scent of Seth's cologne washed over her. He had come up behind her so silently that she hadn't detected his closeness until she felt his warm breath in her ear.

"This is one of my favorite Italian recipes."

"What other dishes do you make?" he asked.

"Through a lot of trial and error I've managed to perfect manicotti, and spinach and mushroom ravioli."

"So, you're a regular Martha Stewart."

Natalia stirred the pot with a wooden spoon to test whether the sauce was thickening. "Not quite."

"You're being modest, Natalia. You've transformed a sterile kitchen you'd normally see in a showroom into one that looks functional and lived-in."

The day before, Natalia had driven to Beckley to browse in the shops where she'd purchased framed prints of flowers, painted glazed pots filled with fresh herbs and an assortment of candles in jars of varying shapes and sizes. Dried hydrangeas overflowed in a blue Depression glass vase on the kitchen tables, and the hutch was filled with bone china, crystal stemware and demitasse cups and saucers.

"It's all about one's personality," she said. "If I'm going to have white walls, then I want contrasting or monochromatic colors." She put the top back on the Dutch oven. "Now that you're here I think we should eat in the dining room."

"Is there anything I can help you with?" Seth asked.

"Would you mind setting the table?"

"Of course not," he said.

When Natalia had invited Seth to share the meal and he'd declined, she could not have contemplated he would change his mind. She had been more than content to cook, eat alone, and then retreat to the living room where she would binge-watch *The Jewel in the Crown*, a series she had inherited from her mother's extensive DVD library.

And she was looking forward to exchanging dishes with Seth. She had always admired men who didn't have to depend on a woman to feed them, and she was also curious as to what he would prepare.

As Natalia gathered the tablecloth, napkins, dishes, serving pieces and glassware Seth needed to set the table, she mused as to how different he was from Daryl, who from their initial meeting had felt the need to challenge, compete and engage in one-upmanship. It should've been a warning that she not agree to see him again, but it had been his selfless dedication to mentoring fatherless youth that allowed her to overlook his negative personality traits.

The other difference between her ex-fiancé and the man in her kitchen was she had no intention of becoming romantically involved with him.

Chapter Five

Natalia parked her car in a lot behind the medical office building. She and Henry Franklin had agreed to meet two hours before they were scheduled to open for the day. She wanted to go over protocol, settle into her office and review patient records.

Exiting the SUV, she walked around to the front of the building and rang the bell. It opened within seconds and she came face-to-face with the man with whom she would work for the next year. Natalia smiled.

"Good morning, Dr. Franklin."

"Good morning and welcome aboard, Dr. Hawkins."

The tall, rail-thin man with graying red hair and twinkling brown eyes in a pale, angular face had been Wickham Falls' family doctor for nearly four decades. When she first sat down with Henry, he'd admitted to hiring her sight unseen because of the recommendation from the chief of staff at the hospital where she'd worked in the ER's trauma unit. And he'd also admired, after he had interviewed her, her decision not to leave the hospital and join her father's practice, but to follow her dream to become a small-town doctor.

"Thank you."

Henry stood off to the side. "Please come in. I don't know if you've had breakfast, but I had my wife fix a little something for us."

"How very thoughtful of her," Natalia said.

She didn't have the heart to tell the man she'd had breakfast before leaving home. The mellow, easygoing camaraderie she'd shared with Seth over dinner had lingered long after he'd helped her clean up the kitchen and then returned home. A Caesar salad, the rigatoni and sausage, warm focaccia bread, along with a couple glasses of red wine had put them in a festive mood where she found herself laughing over nonsensical antics from their childhoods. Before leaving she gave him a glass container with the pasta that he could reheat in the microwave. Natalia's decision not to bring lunch was based on her need to become familiar with the pace of the office.

"We'll eat in the breakroom while I fill you in on the updates we talked about during your interview that you had suggested to counter what had been the organized chaos to which we all had become accustomed," Henry teased.

Natalia was impressed with the physical layout of the medical office. There was the receptionist desk behind a glassed-in partition, and a spacious reception area with a section where children could play until they were seen. Leather seating groupings and low tables with magazines, and a mounted flat-screen TV provided waiting patients with comfort and entertainment. There were two examining rooms, another for X-rays, and a bathroom for patients. There was also a private bathroom and breakroom for the staff. Both she and Henry had offices where they could conduct private consultations.

"I know I may sound a little biased, but I have to say that my wife makes the best blueberry muffins in the county. Whenever we have the Fourth of July bake-off, she wins a prize for best muffins."

Seth had mentioned prizes for best dishes during the town's Independence Day celebration. Natalia had been to state and county fairs, and now she was looking forward to an event where the entire populous turned out to celebrate. And the patriotic fervor was evident by the number of flags attached to lampposts and every storefront.

A slight smile lifted the corners of her mouth when she saw the nameplate on the door to her office. It was obvious Henry had followed through on his promise to add her name to the office letterhead and a supply of lab coats. He had also requested she ship her professional diplomas and licenses before her arrival in order for the workmen to put them on the wall of her office. Natalia had told Henry she wanted to begin seeing patients on her first day.

Once she bit into the still-warm, fluffy blueberry-filled muffin, Natalia knew why Henry had bragged about his wife's baking skill. It was apparent the woman had used fresh berries.

"I take it from your expression that you're enjoying it."

She moaned under her breath as she chewed and swallowed a mouthful of deliciousness. "Oh my goodness! You're right, Henry. This is the best muffin, blueberry aside, I've ever eaten." The older doctor has insisted she call him Henry whenever they were alone because he wasn't one to stand on ceremony.

"I'll definitely let her know that my partner agrees with me."

A slight frown furrowed Natalia's smooth forehead. "Partner?"

Henry nodded. "Yes. I've decided to bring you on as a partner instead of an assistant." He held up his hand when Natalia opened her mouth. "Please let me finish, Natalia. You're probably thinking you have to invest monetarily in the practice, but I won't accept your money. Your advice about bringing the office into the twenty-first century has streamlined the paperwork, reduced staff stress and we're able to get patients in and out a lot more quickly than in the past."

Henry mentioning investing in the practice reminded her of Daryl selling his condo and depleting his savings before becoming a partner at his firm. Making money had become an obsession for him because, unlike Natalia, he'd had to resort to taking out student loans to complete his college and law school education.

Natalia did not want to take advantage of the doctor who'd dedicated more than half his life treating the disadvantaged. "I only suggested the changes to make my life and everyone else's less stressful. So, my motives were purely selfish. And because you won't accept any remuneration from me, then I'm going to suggest you half my salary for the next year." Henry met her eyes, unblinking, in what had become a stare-down.

"Okay, Natalia. But only for one year."

She offered him a warm smile. "Thank you."

With her medical license and experience she was confident enough to know she could have gotten another position with most hospitals in the country or even join her father's practice, except that she'd grown tired of the hustle and bustle of city life. She'd grown up in Paoli, a small town about twenty-five miles outside of Philly with fewer than six thousand inhabitants. Her fondest childhood memories were of her parents driving into Philadelphia to visit a museum or attend a play and then browsing through the Reading Terminal Market. The bright lights and pulse of the city pulled her in and refused to let her go until years later when she had to escape to a place that reminded her of her childhood town.

Henry exhaled an audible breath. "I've left a set of keys to the building and to your office in the desk drawer along with the code to the security system. Only you, I and the receptionist have the security code. There are panic buttons under the receptionist's desk, and in our private offices, to be used in case of a medical emergency. The silent alarm is connected to the sheriff's department who in turn will alert the fire department's emergency medical technicians to transport the patient to the county hospital. And now that you're onboard I'd like to revise our hours but that's something we can discuss and implement by the end of the month."

* * *

That afternoon, Natalia and Henry spent an hour talking about the patients they'd treated and their concerns about the escalation of opiate abuse among the population who had been prescribed painkillers. She had gotten Henry to agree, in lieu of handwriting prescriptions for medications, to email them directly to the local pharmacy. Prescription pads were now under lock and key to prevent anyone from attempting to forge a script.

She retreated to her office and changed out of her street clothes, and into a pair of pale blue scrubs, comfortable shoes and the white lab coat with her name stitched below the medical office's name and logo. She'd just placed her tote in a narrow closet when she heard a knock on the door. Natalia walked over and opened it.

"The staff and I got together to give you this as a welcoming gift."

Natalia's mouth dropped when she saw the receptionist holding a vase filled with a bouquet of colorful flowers. Henry had hired the tall, slender, young military widow and mother of twins, a boy and girl, after his longtime receptionist moved to Delaware to care for her elderly father.

"Thank you so much, Angela. You really didn't have to do this."

Angela Mitchell, a beautiful woman with delicate features in a sable-brown complexion and sporting shoulder-length braided hair, walked into the office and set the bouquet on the credenza. "Yes, we did, Dr. Hawkins." She moved closer to Natalia. "It's not every day we get to see a woman doctor around here. And especially one who is African American."

A warm glow flowed through Natalia. Angela had just confirmed what Natalia told Seth about being a role model for girls or women who looked like her. Satisfaction shimmered in her eyes when she said, "What you've said makes me doubly proud that I decided to become a doctor."

Natalia's first day ended after she saw a steady stream of patients from infants to the elderly. She'd found it a refreshing change from treating gunshot wounds, stabbings and drug overdoses. Rather than being overcome with exhaustion, Natalia felt energized. The recommendations she'd suggested were now in place and had dramatically decreased the wait time for treatment.

All medical records were computerized and when patients arrived they were given a one-page update printout to record their symptoms. The information was uploaded to computers in the exam rooms. Temperatures and blood pressure readings were taken and recorded before the patients were seen by her or Henry. All of the physician notes were entered into the computer, and if necessary, prescriptions for medication were sent electronically to the patient's designated pharmacy.

She pulled into the driveway to her house at the same time she saw Seth alight from an old battered pickup. Natalia had to acknowledge that he looked incredibly handsome in his uniform. "Good evening, neighbor," she called out.

Seth approached Natalia. "Good evening to you, too. How was your first day?"

* * *

His gaze took in everything about her in one, sweeping glance. There was something about his neighbor that had him thinking about her when he least expected. He wasn't certain whether it was the sound of her dulcet voice that held him captive or her ability to make him feel completely at ease in her presence. Seth knew he'd overstayed his welcome the night before because he'd so enjoyed her company that he hadn't wanted to go home.

The women he saw once his divorce was finalized were temporary distractions. A few he liked enough to ask for a second date but none since Melissa, his ex-wife, intrigued him like Natalia.

Even Natalia's laugh reminded him of Melissa's. Although Seth had acknowledged being away from home for extended periods of time was to blame for the breakup of his marriage, she should've communicated to him that she wanted out before seeking to assuage her loneliness by sleeping with one of his fellow marines.

"It was interesting," Natalia said. "And yours?"

Seth angled his head. "Thankfully it was quiet. The only excitement was when I heated up your rigatoni and sausage and everyone wanted to sample it because of the incredible aroma."

She smiled. "What did you do?"

"I went into my office, closed and locked the door and didn't come out until I'd finished eating."

"Haven't you heard of sharing?" Natalia teased.

"There wasn't enough to share. I'm going to put some veggies and Cornish hens on the grill and I'm hoping you'll come and eat with me." When he told

Natalia that he had to step up his game when it came to cooking, he'd gone online and pulled up recipes for poultry. He found one that recommended he marinate the tiny birds in low-sodium soy sauce, ginger, honey, green onions and orange zest before either roasting or grilling them.

Natalia paused. "Can I get a rain check?"

Seth successfully hid his disappointment behind a forced smile. "Sure."

"I've eaten so much today that I don't want to see another morsel. Dr. Franklin ordered a buffet lunch for the staff, and there are enough leftovers for at least another two days."

"Perhaps, then, another time," he asked. Seth knew he wouldn't have another opportunity to spend time with Natalia until the weekend. Once Roger returned, he would go back to his regular schedule.

"I'm looking forward to it," Natalia said, smiling. "Later."

He waited for Natalia to go inside her house, and then retreated to his. He disengaged the security system and tossed his house and truck keys in the sweet-grass basket he'd bought at a stand on a highway in Savannah. Sitting on a low bench, Seth took off his boots, left them on a mat and walked on sock-covered feet up the staircase to his bedroom. He removed the nine-millimeter handgun from his holster and placed it in the safe on an overhead shelf in the walk-in closet alongside a smaller off-duty automatic. Filling in for Roger meant he had to be in bed earlier than usual in order to begin work at dawn. He'd stepped into the role as acting sheriff as if he'd performed it every day. Rising to the rank of master sergeant in the Corps had prepared him to issue orders and expect them to be followed without question. Andy had come by the station house and Seth told him in no uncertain terms that he was not to return to duty without medical clearance. Andy's resentment of Seth occupying the office in Roger's absence was palpable but he refused to back down or submit to intimidation. Eighteen years as a Marine Corps military police officer had developed him into a formidable and fearless foe. It was something Andy immediately recognized when he turned on his heel, and then walked out.

He changed out of his khaki uniform, leaving it and the two-way radio and gun belt on the window seat, and slipped into a pair of jogging pants, a T-shirt and running shoes. Inviting Natalia to come over to eat with him in his home would be a first for Seth since his return to Wickham Falls. It had been nearly two years since he'd made the decision to settle down in the place of his birth, and in all that time no woman other than his mother and sisters had slept under his roof. And those he slept with were far enough away from The Falls where the likelihood of them being seen together was slim to none. The town was too small and he was too well-known to carry on a liaison with a woman that wouldn't garner talk.

Seth went down to the kitchen and removed the hens and asparagus spears wrapped in prosciutto he'd prepped the night before to bring them to room temperature. He waited for the spring, summer and fall months to cook outdoors. Everything went on the gas grill: meat, fish, vegetables and fruit. The only time he used the kitchen was during the winter. His father's last major project before he retired and hung up his tool belt was to remodel the gourmet kitchen. It had taken Adam Collier nearly a month to replace the floor, put up backsplashes and install counter-tops and cabinets. Once the refrigerator-freezer, dishwasher, stove with eye-level ovens and microwave were operable, it took more than a week for his wife to prepare a meal in her new kitchen. She'd become so accustomed to using the gas grill that she admitted she preferred cooking outdoors—especially in the warmer weather.

Ninety minutes later, the aroma of grilled food lingered in the air, and as Seth sat on the top step of the back porch staring out at the fence separating his property from those on the next street, a feeling of peace swept over him and he wondered why he had stayed away for so long. He could have fulfilled his dream to become involved in law enforcement without joining the military. He could've gone to college and selected criminal justice as his major and subsequently applied to the county or state police. Chances are by this time he would've married a local girl, bought a house and had a family.

Extending his legs, Seth closed his eyes, inhaled a lungful of air, held it and then let it out slowly. He did not want to think about what could've been but instead plan to make the best of his future. Although he lived alone he wasn't lonely. There were guys who were in his high school graduating class with whom he'd maintained contact. Most of them were married and were always attempting to hook him up with a woman looking for a "good guy." He liked to think of himself as a good guy and more than able to find his own woman.

Seth pushed to his feet and walked into the house when fireflies flitted about as dusk descended over the countryside. No more staying up and watching late-night TV. He had to begin his workday at six.

Seth's instincts kicked in when he spied the driver of the van with Tennessee plates driving recklessly. After two weeks, he was back to his regular shift and it felt good to get out of the station house where he alternated driving around to the different neighborhoods with the foot patrols.

Activating the lights on the cruiser, he accelerated until he came alongside the van. Instead of slowing the driver of the van sped up. Seth turned on the siren and the chase was on.

"Clown," he swore under his breath. There was no way a minivan could outrun a police cruiser. The pursuit continued until they neared the town limit for Wickham Falls and Seth knew he had to act quickly or he would leave his jurisdiction. He maneuvered closer to the other vehicle's rear bumper and turned his wheel sharply to the right and made contact. The van spun around and rolled over as the driver lost control, the vehicle ending upside down in a ditch on the side of the road.

Seth was out of his car, gun in hand as he cautiously approached the driver's side of the vehicle. Within seconds he assessed the situation. The man's head lay at an awkward angle against the headrest. Reaching into the open window Seth pressed his fingers to the side of his neck, feeling for a pulse. The driver was still alive.

He switched on the radio attached to his left shoulder and reported his location and that he needed an ambulance and a tow truck. Seth took out his handcuffs and cuffed the injured man's left hand to the wheel. It was only after he slid back the doors and inspected the van's cargo compartment that he understood why the driver had tried to get away when he opened one of three cartons filled with boxes of fentanyl. Then he made another call, this time to the state police. He informed the person who'd answered the phone what he'd discovered and suggested they contact the local DEA office.

EMTs from Wickham Falls arrived at the same time as the state police. Motorists were slowing, some videotaping the scene of marked and unmarked police cars, and nearly a dozen law enforcement officers. Special agents from the FBI were contacted because the driver, who would probably be charged as a drug trafficker, had crossed state lines. Seth leaned against his cruiser, answering questions from each of the authorities as cartons of the drug were off-loaded and placed into the trunks of personnel from drug enforcement who'd estimated the haul had netted approximately two thousand pills.

Roger arrived, along with a reporter and camera people from the local television station. When Seth refused to be interviewed, Roger stepped in as the spokesperson for the Wickham Falls' sheriff department. He affected a serious expression as he bragged that his deputy was responsible for catching a trafficker before he could flood the region with more opioids.

Two hours before he was scheduled to clock out

for the night, Roger ordered Seth to go home and relax, that he was proud of his newest deputy and that the mayor and town council were planning to give him a special commendation for his exemplary police work.

Seth, not willing to argue with his superior officer, nodded and got into his cruiser and drove back to the station house parking lot. He still couldn't get the image of a child's car seat out of his mind when he first approached the minivan, thinking he'd run a vehicle off the road with a baby or small child inside. He hadn't realized he'd been holding his breath until he saw that the driver was alone.

Natalia stood up when she heard the approaching vehicle. Within minutes Seth had backed the pickup into the driveway. Word had spread quickly throughout the town about deputy sheriff Seth Collier's quick thinking in apprehending a man bringing opioids into the state.

"Hey, super crime fighter," she teased when Seth stepped out.

His head popped up and he stared at her as if he hadn't seen her before. "How's it going?"

Natalia saw the lines bracketing his strong mouth that hadn't been there before. The buoyant mood vanished like someone letting the air out of a balloon. She left the porch and approached him. "I should be the one asking how you are."

"Other than wound a little too tight, I'm good. I suppose you heard about what happened near Mineral Springs."

"Yes. Someone came into the office just before we closed and couldn't stop talking about the car chase and you running someone off the road who had a car filled with pills." She rested a hand on his upper arm. The muscles under his uniform blouse were hard as cement. "Do you want me to give you something to help you to relax?"

Seth shook his head. "No, thanks. All I need right now is a hot shower, a couple shots of tequila and a firm bed to help me relax. And when I wake up tomorrow, I'll feel like a new man."

"I recommend a massage instead of the tequila if you don't want to run the risk of waking up with a hangover."

"And where would I find a masseuse this time of night?"

"After you take your shower, I'll give you a massage."

Seth's eyebrows lifted. "You?"

Natalia smiled. "Yes, me. I am a doctor and I can assure you that I'm more than familiar with the six hundred and forty muscles in the human body. It's the least I can do for our hometown hero who's responsible for arresting someone transporting drugs that are destroying people's lives."

"*Our* hometown?"

A soft laugh escaped her parted lips. "Yes, 'our,' Seth. I also live here and so far I haven't had to treat anyone addicted to drugs. And I'd like to keep it that way." Natalia thought of herself as fortunate that since she'd begun working with Henry, none of her patients exhibited any signs of drug abuse or addiction.

"Okay, Dr. Hawkins," Seth said, smiling. "You've got yourself a client. Or should I say a patient?"

She returned his smile. "Either will do. I'll leave the door unlocked. Just come over whenever you're ready."

Chapter Six

Seth lay facedown, on a pillow on the dining room table. Natalia had put down a sheet and several pillows to cushion the hard surface, and another sheet covered his half-naked body. She'd waited until he'd stripped down to his boxer briefs and lay down before she entered the room, perhaps to permit him a modicum of modesty.

He wasn't her patient, didn't want to be but as someone who was interested in her as a man was in a woman. Seth had conveniently kept his distance from Natalia, despite their living next door to each other, arriving home when she was probably in or preparing to go to bed, and leaving to go on duty when she was at her office. In the past he hadn't been so hesitant when it came to letting a woman know he was interested in her but somehow it was different with

Natalia. Instinct told him he had to go slowly and cautiously because he suspected she'd been emotionally scarred by her ex-fiancé. She'd admitted that she had *just* gotten rid of her fiancé and wasn't looking for a boyfriend, which seemed to imply that the breakup had to have been recent.

"Close your eyes and breathe slowly," Natalia said in his ear as she leaned over him. "I'm going to start with your occipitalis, the muscles pulling the scalp toward the back, and slowly work my way down to the short peroneus. That's the muscle attached to the fibula that enables the foot to extend and to draw away from the median axis of the body."

He chuckled under his breath. "Whatever you say, Doctor. It all sounds good to me."

"You're going to have to tell me what makes you uncomfortable because I'm going to apply pressure to stimulate the deeper muscles and surrounding tissues."

Seth lost track of time as he was transported to another dimension when he felt himself succumbing to the ministrations of Natalia's magical fingers kneading and loosening knots in his neck, shoulders, arms, legs and finally his feet.

"Wake up, Seth."

He hadn't realized he'd fallen asleep when she shook him gently. He opened his eyes and lifted his head. "How long was I out?"

"Probably about half an hour." Natalia curved an arm around his shoulders and assisted him to sit upright. "How do you feel?"

Seth rolled his head from side to side. "Like a new man." He could not remember when he'd felt this relaxed. His eyes moved slowly over Natalia's face and came to rest on her mouth—a mouth he longed to take in a long, deep kiss. Everything about her seeped into him: her warmth, the natural scent of her body and the subtle fragrance of perfume. "Your hands should be registered as a controlled substance. They cause drowsiness, dizziness and I will have to use extreme caution when operating a vehicle, vessel or machine," he teased.

Natalia rested a hand on his shoulder. "I hope you're not talking about driving tonight."

"No." His intent was to go home and straight to bed. "How much do I owe you, Dr. Hawkins?"

"A home-cooked meal," she said, repeating what he'd told her what now seemed so long ago.

He winked at her. "All right! If that's the case, then are you busy Saturday?"

"We have hours until one, and after that I'm free."

He leaned closer until their mouths were mere inches apart. "If the weather holds, then we can cook and dine outdoors. After that, if you're not too full, we'll go for a drive and I'll give you a guided tour of *our* beautiful countryside."

Natalia lowered her eyes. "Do you want me to bring anything?"

"Yes."

"What?"

Seth angled his head and kissed her cheek. "You. All I'll need is you."

Natalia's intake and exhalation of breath echoed in his ear. "Are you certain you don't want me to bring dessert?"

He pressed his cheek to hers. "Very certain." Seth

knew he had to get off the table, put on his clothes and go home because he was becoming aroused under the top sheet, and that was something he didn't want Natalia to see. "Could you please give me my jeans?" Natalia picked them off the chair and handed them to him. "Thank you."

"Would you like some water?"

Seth quickly pushed his legs into the denim fabric and pulled them up over his hips. He reached for the T-shirt and put it on. "No, thank you." He followed her into the kitchen, watching as she filled a glass from the in-door water dispenser. "You were right that a massage is better than a shot of tequila."

She peered at him over the glass. "Didn't you mention two shots?"

"Yes, I did. Again, I thank you for making me feel better without having to face the possibility of a hangover."

Natalia took a swallow of water, and then set the glass on the countertop. "I'm glad I could help."

He'd experienced a jolt of adrenaline during the high-speed car chase that had continued once he discovered the drugs. But once personnel from the different law enforcement agencies arrived, his euphoria plummeted like an addict coming down off his or her high. The answers to questions he'd had to repeat over and over pelted him like tiny missiles and all he wanted was to leave the scene to the DEA and FBI.

Seth beckoned to Natalia. "Please come walk me to the door and lock it after me."

Natalia approached him and took his hand. "Are you prepared for the all of the attention from those who are calling you a hero crime fighter?"

He pondered her question as they walked. "I'm far from being a hero. I just did what I'm paid to do and that is to protect and serve The Falls. The guy would've gotten away if I hadn't noticed him driving recklessly. And if he'd stopped when I signaled for him to pull over, I probably would've given him a warning because he had out of state plates."

"Would you have inspected his vehicle?"

"I don't know," Seth said truthfully. "Even if he'd lied and said he was exhausted because he'd been driving for hours and that he was going to stop and check in at a motel off the interstate, I probably would've believed him. And he had to have been insane to think a swagger wagon could outrun a police cruiser."

Natalia giggled like a little girl. "No, you didn't say swagger wagon."

Seth's deep laugh joined hers. "Well, it was a minivan." He sobered. "Once I forced it off the road and saw the child's car seat, I nearly lost it because I feared there had been a child inside the car."

"Thankfully there wasn't."

He nodded. "You're right." Seth lowered his head and dropped a kiss on Natalia's short hair. "Good night and thank you again for the massage."

"Good night, Seth."

Natalia closed and locked the door behind Seth. She felt as if she'd been holding her breath the instant Seth shed his clothes and lay on the table with only a pair of briefs covering his nakedness. She had lost count since she'd entered medical school the number of times she'd viewed the nude male body. However, she had learned to compartmentalize to separate the two into different categories: one for medicine and the other for sexual pleasure. And there was no doubt she had categorized Seth in the latter.

She knew it had been a while since she'd made love with a man and as a woman with normal sexual desires, Natalia wondered how much longer she would continue to deny her needs. Once she knew her relationship with Daryl was on shaky ground they had stopped making love. There was no way she could share her body with a man with whom she had ongoing arguments, coupled with the fact that she was so exhausted from the long hours she spent in the ER that all she wanted when she returned home was to catch up on her sleep.

Daryl and the double shifts were in her past and despite her prior protest to Seth that she wasn't looking to get into another relationship, she had changed her stance. He was the complete opposite of the men who'd expressed an interest in her and usually came on so strong that it turned her off. It wasn't vanity that indicated Seth wanted to spend time with her but what she liked about him was that he was willing to let her take the lead.

And aside from his incredibly handsome face and spectacular body, she admired his modesty. Word had traveled quickly in Wickham Falls when folks reported that Seth refused to be interviewed, which left Roger to represent the sheriff's department. She and the staff had gathered on Main Street along with throngs of the curious when affiliates from several national television stations set up to cover what had become a major drug bust. What was earlier purported to be two thousand pills was confirmed to be closer to twenty thousand. Once agents from the DEA examined the van and found more boxes hidden beneath three rows of seats, they claimed it a major victory in the effort to stem the illegal sale of fentanyl.

A slow smile parted her lips when she turned and walked into the dining room to remove the bedding from the table. Her sexy neighbor was definitely someone she could consider as a boyfriend. It had been less than five months since she and Daryl broke up and she needed at least six months before she could consider dating again.

She hadn't thought that when she had agreed to relocate from Pennsylvania to West Virginia she would move next door to a man she didn't want to lump in the same category as her ex. There were times when she'd imagined Daryl felt he was doing her a favor by dating her, when she realized it was the complete opposite. Even before she had become involved with him, there were a number of men who'd asked her out but her vow not to date anyone with whom she worked ruled them out. And now that she looked back Natalia realized she had been too rigid and that pledges were made to be broken.

"Dr. Hawkins, your next patient is in exam room two." The medical assistant's voice shattered Natalia's concentration as she attempted to finish reading an article on heart disease published in a medical journal.

Natalia tapped a button on the intercom. "Thank you, Leah." Henry had been called away to make a house call, which left her with the sole responsibility of seeing patients until his return. In the past, when he had to leave the office, the receptionist would call patients to inform them Dr. Franklin was running late or to reschedule them for another day and time. Natalia had made it a practice to come in at least an hour early to review the files for all of the patients scheduled for the day.

She glanced at the name of the patient on her desktop, left the office, walked across the hall and pushed open the door. She saw a young mother sitting on a chair bouncing a raven-haired toddler on her lap.

Natalia smiled at a woman with a mane of brown, reddish-tipped curls framing a tawny-gold complexion and ending above her shoulders. "Mrs. Wainwright. I'm Dr. Hawkins. Dr. Franklin had to step out, so I'll be taking care of Lily today."

"I know who you are, Dr. Hawkins. I'm Mya and we're practically neighbors."

An expression of confusion crossed Natalia's features. "We are?"

"Yes. I live across the road from you and Seth Collier. Seth and my husband have become good friends because both of them were in the Marines."

Natalia's dark eyes met Mya's large hazel ones. She extended her hand. "It's nice meeting you, neighbor. I'm Natalia."

Mya shook Natalia's hand. "I'd planned to come and introduce myself, but I didn't want to impose."

"Believe me, you would not have been an imposition. I've lived here for two weeks and the only folks I've interacted with, aside from Seth, are patients."

"Even though I grew up here and I'm a stay-at-home mom I rarely find time to do much socializing."

Natalia nodded. "Taking care of a toddler is

definitely a full-time job." She glanced over at the computer with Lily's medical record. The medical assistant, Leah Perry, had entered the little girl's temperature, height, weight and blood pressure, checked her eyes, ears, throat, heart and lungs—all of which were within normal range for her age. "What brings Lily in today?"

"We're going to the Bahamas next week, and I'm a couple of months past due getting Lily's second dose of hepatitis A."

"It's good you brought her in," Natalia said as she washed her hands in the stainless-steel sink and then slipped on a pair of examining gloves. "You can place her on the table and pull down her pants to her knees." As Mya readied her daughter for the injection, Natalia removed a vial with the vaccine from a locked drawer, shook it vigorously and inserted a hypodermic into the solution, and slipped the needle into the pocket of her lab coat. She had performed the task without letting Lily see what was to come.

She stared at the child with clear, sky-blue eyes and inky black hair. Lily looked nothing like her mother and Natalia assumed she must resemble her father. "Oh my, you have such pretty eyes." Lily stared without blinking as her tiny rosebud mouth tightened noticeably. She clung to her mother's arm.

"Most of the time she's a chatterbox," Mya admitted.

"Many children are traumatized by doctors." Natalia leaned closer and when she sang the nursery rhyme the "Itsy Bitsy Spider," Lily joined in. It was obvious she was familiar with the song. Meanwhile Natalia swabbed an area on the toddler's thigh with alcohol and, in a motion almost too quick for the eye to follow, injected the vaccine.

Lily barely had time to react and stopped singing, her eyes filling with tears. "No!"

Mya kissed her daughter's silky curling hair. "It's over, sweetheart." Lily sniffled loudly, but didn't cry. "Thank you," she whispered, smiling at Natalia. "She's always hysterical after getting a shot."

"A little distraction usually does the trick to take her mind off what is to come. Another ploy is not to let the patient see the hypodermic beforehand."

"I'm glad it worked with Lily," Mya said. "We're going to New York for a few days before flying down to the Caribbean, but plan to come back in time for the holiday weekend. I'd like for you to join Giles and me at our table for the Memorial Day picnic following the parade. The townsfolk always gather under a gigantic tent on the church lawn for an afternoon of music, fun and games."

Natalia felt a warm glow flow through her with the invitation. She had heard talk about the holiday festivities, but Mya was the first one to invite her to celebrate it with her family. She wanted to ask Mya if Seth was going to join them because she'd mention his connection to her husband. "I'd loved to join you, and thank you for asking."

Mya waved her left hand and the overhead light reflected off the diamond eternity band on her finger. "My motives for asking are purely selfish because I'm curious as to why you decided to practice medicine in Wickham Falls when your license plate reads Pennsylvania."

Natalia discarded the needle in the red canister for used hypodermics. "That's a long story."

"Well, if you ever need someone to talk to then just walk across the road and ring the bell. Giles divides his time between The Falls, New York and the Bahamas for business, so there are times when it's just me and Lily."

Natalia wanted to remind Mya that she was the one with a husband and child and she didn't believe in just dropping by unannounced. "That goes both ways. If you feel the need for some adult female company, then you're more than welcome to come over with Lily." Reaching for the prescription pad, she jotted down her cell phone number. "Call me and let me know when you're free." Mya's eyes sparkled like multicolored gemstones when she smiled, and Natalia wondered if perhaps she was experiencing bouts of loneliness because of her husband's business trips.

"I will." She pulled up Lily's pants and set her on her feet. "Since you were such a good girl, Mommy's going to take you out for ice cream."

"I like ice cream, Mommy."

"I know you do." Mya winked at Natalia.

She updated Lily's chart with the date and type of vaccine. "Lily is up to date on all of her immunizations. However, she'll need a fifth dose of DTaP to protect her from diphtheria, tetanus, whooping cough, a second dose of MMR for protection against measles, mumps and German measles, and Varicella for chicken pox between the ages of four and six, and before she enters school. I've flagged her chart and we have your email address, so we'll send out a reminder once she celebrates her fourth birthday." Tapping a key, she sent the information to Angela's computer for the receptionist to print out and file in the patient's folder.

"We're leaving, sweetheart," Mya said when Lily tugged on her slacks. "I'm so glad the office is now computerized. In the past we got postcards reminding us of appointments."

"It makes life easier for everyone involved." Natalia waved to the little girl. "Bye, Lily. Have a safe trip."

Lily peered around her mother's leg. "Bye."

Natalia waited for them to leave and then picked up the phone. "Who's next, Leah?"

"Mr. Sanderson is in room one."

"Thanks." She walked out as Leah came in to change the paper on the examining table. Since Natalia had reorganized the office protocol everything worked more smoothly. It had taken less than a week before everyone had become familiar as to their function and the waiting area was no longer crowded with patients waiting beyond their appointed time to be seen.

Natalia walked in, introduced herself and shook hands with the man who'd complained of pain in his right knee. "I'm going to have the technician take an X-ray of your knee to see what I'm working with," she said, as she washed her hands.

Although the X-rays were negative he asked if she could prescribe a painkiller to ease his discomfort. "I'm sorry, Mr. Sanderson, I can't do that. I recommend you take an over-the-counter pain reliever, and if your pain continues, then I'll give you a referral for an MRI."

He walked out, shouting that she wasn't a real doctor, but Natalia wasn't bothered by his outburst. She suspected he wanted her to write a script for a narcotic pain reliever either for his personal use or someone else. The opioid epidemic gripping the country was a crisis and she refused to add to it by arbitrarily prescribing drugs to anyone complaining of pain.

By the time Henry returned, she'd diagnosed and treated an eight-year-old with conjunctivitis and a teenage boy with strep throat. Natalia still was getting used to working shorter hours and arriving home in time to unwind, prepare dinner for herself and get a head start on housework.

She wasn't certain when it started, but she found herself sitting on the porch or in the living room listening for the sound of Seth's pickup before going to bed. Most times he returned home between ten thirty and eleven, and the one night he didn't arrive until after midnight she whispered a silent prayer that he was safe. What she did not want to acknowledge was that she was not only attracted to him but she also liked him—a lot.

The rain that had begun Friday night continued into Saturday, with meteorologists predicting it not to end until Sunday, and Natalia doubted whether Seth would be able to cook outdoors. She and Henry had agreed to alternate working on Saturdays, and with a retired school nurse, they saw patients who were unable to come during weekdays. Revised office hours were now nine to six Monday through Friday, nine to one on Saturday. The rain was coming down in torrents when she locked the door behind the nurse minutes before noon. There were two cancellations and she decided to wait until one to see if she would have a walk-in.

The telephone rang and she picked up the receiver before the second ring. "First Care Medical."

"Dr. Hawkins, this is deputy sheriff Seth Collier."

She sat up straight. It was the first time she and Seth had spoken over the phone. "How are you?"

"I'm right as rain."

Natalia rolled her eyes upward. "Please don't mention rain. Do you think we should start building an ark?" she teased.

Seth's laugh caressed her ear. "Nah. It's been pretty dry around here, so we need the rain. By the way, May is our rainiest month. And I don't mind it because it keeps the troublemakers indoors. I'm calling to ask if you wouldn't mind accompanying me to a restaurant in Charleston later on this evening instead of eating at home."

"Deputy Collier, are you asking me out on a date?"

"Yes, I am."

Slumping back in the chair, Natalia stared at the diplomas on the wall above the credenza cradling photographs of her with friends and family. She'd had a hard and fast rule not to date until six months after her last breakup, but apparently Seth asking her out was going to change that.

"Okay."

"Okay what, Natalia?"

"I'd love to go out with you."

"Love?"

"Stop it! You know what I mean," she countered.

Seth chuckled again. "I should let you know that

I'm very literal. To me, love is a lot stronger an emotion than like."

"Like, like, like," Natalia said over and over. "I'd like to go out with you tonight."

"That's better. I'll make a reservation for seven, so can you be ready to leave at six?"

"Yes. I'll see you later." Natalia replaced the receiver in the handset, picked up a pen and drew interlocking circles on a pad that had a drug company logo.

Seth had asked whether she could be ready when Daryl had demanded she be ready. And it wasn't until she was free of him that she wondered if she'd lost her senses when she surrendered her will to a man who felt he had the right to program her life.

Daryl's attempt to control her life had been so subtle that Natalia wasn't aware of what was happening until her mother pointed it out to her. Sylvia Hawkins had pulled her aside after a family reunion and asked her in Spanish why she had allowed Daryl to speak for her whenever someone asked her a question about her future. She'd wondered why her mother had spoken to her in the language she'd taught her children when they very young, but when she turned around, she'd discovered Daryl had followed them in an attempt to eavesdrop on their conversation.

In that instant it was as if a lightbulb had been turned on and she saw the man with whom she'd pledged her future in a whole new light. She'd asked Daryl to excuse himself while she spoke to her mother and when he hesitated she raised her voice ordering him to leave. Later that evening when they returned home she told him in no uncertain terms that if he ever attempted to spy on her again, then it was better they stop seeing each other. Then Daryl did what he could do best—become remorseful and apologetic.

Two weeks later when Natalia drove to Paoli to have lunch with her mother they talked at length about her and Daryl. Her mother had asked whether she was in love with him or in love with his meteoric rise as one of Philadelphia's brilliant young litigators. Sylvia's query left Natalia where she'd begun to question her feelings about the man whose ring she wore. The four-carat ring Daryl had selected without her input and one she rarely wore except when they went out together socially. Time and time again she tried to have compassion for her fiancé's drive for success and perfection because of his underprivileged childhood but in the end she knew he had to stop compensating for something which he had no control over.

Pushing back her chair, she stood and walked over to the window. Her office faced the rear parking lot. Many of the spaces were empty and she attributed that to the inclement weather. Natalia had learned quickly that parking rules were strictly enforced. Members of the town council had voted to install meters along Main Street, and parking behind stores and shops was limited to two-hour intervals. An area had been designated employee-only parking. Shopkeepers were required to complete an application for a nominal fee and file it with copies of their workers' car registrations to get stickers that employees had to affix to the bumpers of their vehicles. Natalia and Henry, along with the postmaster, the fire and sheriff's departments, and town hall personnel, were issued special vehicle permits as first responders. Overnight parking in the downtown business district was prohibited between the hours of two and six. Parking violations became a source of revenue for the town treasurer.

Not only was the rain coming down in sheets it was also blowing sideways, and Natalia doubted whether anyone was going to show up unless they had a medical emergency. She'd just closed the window blinds and turned off the table lamps when the phone rang again. "First Care Medical. This is Dr. Hawkins."

"Seth again."

Her eyebrows lifted slightly. "Are you calling to cancel our date?"

"Not really. I just heard on the police scanner that a section of the road leading to the interstate has been washed out, and I wanted to ask whether you'd rather come to my place for dinner."

She smiled. "Are you still talking about grilling outdoors?"

"No. But I need to know if you're allergic to shellfish."

"No. Why?" she asked.

"I'd like to serve surf and turf. I have an electric indoor smokeless grill."

"Count me in but only if I can make the sides."

"You're in, babe."

"What time do you want me to come over?"

"Anytime you want. I'm not going out."

Natalia estimated it would take her time to stop at the supermarket to get the items she needed for the sides to go along with the fish and steak. "If that's the case then look for me sometime this afternoon."

"It's going to be fun to cook together."

"We'll see about that, chef," she said teasingly.

Seth laughed. "Yes, we will."

Natalia ended the call, slipped on her rain slicker and gathered her tote. Normally she would've changed out of the scrubs and into jeans and a T-shirt. She armed the security system, locked the door and headed for the parking lot. If it hadn't been raining she would've walked down to the supermarket, but not today because she would be soaked through to the skin before reaching her car.

She was in and out of the market within fifteen minutes. The clerk complained she hadn't checked out more than twenty people since they opened the doors at eight because of the weather. Natalia started the SUV remotely, slipped in behind the wheel and turned the wipers to the fastest setting. She exhaled an audible sigh of relief when she finally maneuvered into the driveway of her house. Many of the roads were flooding because the rain was coming down so fast and heavy that drains weren't able to handle the overflow.

Walking around to the back of the house, she opened the door and walked into the combination mud-laundry room. After hanging the slicker on a wall hook, Natalia slipped out of her shoes, and stripped down to her underwear. Walking on bare feet, she made her way to the bathroom. She needed a cup of tea and a shower, but not necessarily in that order. After that, she planned to gather the ingredients she needed to make the sides for dinner with Seth.

Chapter Seven

Natalia bit back a smile when Seth opened the door and went completely still. They were similarly dressed in faded jeans and sweatshirts. Hers with a logo of her college alma mater and his stamped with the insignia of the seal of the US Marine Corps.

"May I come in?"

"Yes. Of course," he said, at the same time he took the two large canvas bags from her loose grip. Seth peered into one of the bags. "What on earth did you buy?"

Natalia kicked off her running shoes and left them on the mat inside the door. "Everything I need to make coleslaw and duchess potatoes."

"What the heck are duchess potatoes?"

She strolled past him and into the living room. "You'll see." The open floor plan with a great room that combined the kitchen, dining room and living room gave the illusion of a much larger space. "I like the furnishings and layout of your home."

"I can't take credit for any of it. My father renovated the entire house the year he retired, while my sister who is an interior decorator selected all of the furnishings."

"She's quite talented."

The full charm came from uncluttered simplicity and unimposing furniture with a wingback chair and a classic, long, curved-arm sofa. The style was a combination of country and contemporary. Cheery yellow walls provided a cool backdrop for shades of beige and teal upholstery and natural wood. Natalia ran her fingers over the back of the wing chair covered with a teal fabric that had a raised crewel texture.

Seth glanced at Natalia over his shoulder. He set the bags on the stools at the breakfast bar. "I know I may sound biased because Julie's my sister, but she's incredibly gifted. As a student at SCAD, the Savannah College of Art and Design, she won a number of awards for her ability to mix styles and textures. I remember her saying she wanted to blend a Shaker influence, whatever that means, with early-American pieces and contemporary when my mother said she wanted an informal country look, while Dad preferred furniture that was more modern-day."

"Do you like it?" Natalia asked.

Seth turned to meet her eyes. "I love it. There's nothing in this house I'd change." He paused. "Do you like it?"

A slow smile parted her lips. "Yes."

His smile matched hers. "Good. After we eat, I'll

give you a tour of upstairs and the basement. Now, come and show me what you brought."

Natalia wasn't certain why Seth wanted to know what she thought of his home, but apparently he was pleased with her response. She emptied from the bag onto the cooking island plastic bags filled with small heads of red and green cabbage, potatoes, eggs, a container of cream, grated Parmesan cheese, carrots, celery, white onion and red pepper, a jar of mayonnaise, white wine vinegar, Dijon mustard and paprika.

"Damn," Seth drawled under his breath. "You need all of this for your sides?"

"Yes. I must say I like the Village Market. It may not be as large as supermarkets like Kroger's, but they stock everything I need to make my favorite dishes." Natalia emptied the other bag she had filled with utensils, baking sheets and cookware.

"You didn't have to bring a baking sheet. I have a few."

"This is my first time in your home, so I wasn't sure what you had."

Seth knew Natalia was right. It was her first time—he hoped it wouldn't be her last—and she was the only woman to cross the threshold since his return.

"Do you need a sous chef?" he asked when Natalia slipped on a bibbed apron with two large pockets.

"Thanks for asking, but I have everything under control."

Seth sat watching as she wielded a knife with the skill of a trained chef as she finely shredded cabbage and carrots, and chopped a stalk of celery, white onion and the small red pepper into a bowl for the slaw. She filled a separate bowl with mayonnaise, a couple tablespoons of white wine vinegar and a teaspoon of Dijon, and whisked them before tossing the dressing with the vegetables. She covered the bowl with something that looked to Seth like a colorful shower cap.

"That works a lot better than plastic wrap," he remarked.

Natalia nodded. "I bought these food covers after I got fed up cutting myself on the metal edge on plastic wrap boxes. They're washable and microwave safe." She handed him the bowl. "Please put this in the fridge."

Seth placed the bowl on a shelf in the refrigerator and then returned to watch Natalia peel potatoes. "How long will it take for you to make duchess potatoes?"

"Twenty minutes once they're ready for baking. I'm going to put them in a bowl of cold water until I'm ready to boil them."

"What do you want to drink?"

Natalia smiled as she washed the potatoes. "What are the choices?"

"I have beer, wine, water, bourbon and whiskey."

Throwing back her head, she laughed. "I'll take wine."

"Red or white?"

"If we're having steak, then I'll have red."

Slipping off the stool, Seth walked to a door in the streamlined kitchen and opened it. "Pinot noir or merlot?"

Natalia washed and then dried her hands on a towel as she stared numbly at the pullout shelves in the neatly stocked pantry. There were compartments for cans, packaged food, bottled water, juice and another one for paper goods.

"How genius," she said breathlessly. "Did your father install these, too?"

Seth flashed a sheepish grin. "No. I did last year." He opened the door under the cabinets to reveal pull-out shelves with pots, bowls and small kitchen appliances. "I got tired of opening a cabinet and having to search for pots and lids."

"It's amazing that you have everything within reach."

"For me it's a time-saver."

Natalia thought installing the custom pullout shelves in the existing cabinets was ingenious. It had allowed Seth more access to what he needed within minutes. "You've must really enjoy cooking here."

"I do on my days off in the winter."

"I felt the same way when I was on staff at the hospital. Whenever I had a couple of days off I'd spend the time preparing all of my favorite dishes and then pack them away in storage containers to heat up whenever I came home after working double shifts."

Seth opened a drawer for a corkscrew and deftly removed the cork from the wine bottle. He poured a small amount into a wineglass and handed it to her. "Let me know if you like it."

She took a sip. "It's perfect."

He poured more wine into her glass and then filled his. "Here's to an enjoyable evening that I hope is the beginning of many more to come."

Natalia touched her glass to his. "Hear! Hear!"

Seth walked over to the opposite end of the kitchen and opened the door to an overhead cabinet and switched on the audio component. Music flowed throughout the space from wireless speakers concealed throughout the first story.

He returned to the cooking island, bent slightly from the waist and extended his hand. "Will you do me the honor of dancing with me?"

She took a sip of wine as if to fortify herself to resist what she'd refused to acknowledge from the first time she stared into the smiling eyes of her neighbor. Natalia found everything about him appealing and that posed a problem for her. She'd just gotten out of a relationship that left her wary of the opposite sex only to move less than a hundred feet from a man whose very presence reminded her that she was a woman with normal physical needs.

Natalia moved into his embrace and rested her head on his shoulder. She closed her eyes and silently surrendered to the man who could take her breath away with a mere smile, and whose virility had lingered with her even when they were apart.

"I like this song," she said softly. It was "The Dance," featuring BeBe Winans from the Dave Koz album of the same name.

Seth buried his face in her short hair. "Me, too. It's a favorite of mine."

They danced together barely moving their feet and Natalia felt the tiny shivers of gooseflesh rising on her arms under the sweatshirt. The song ended and she eased back to look up at him staring down at her.

Seth lowered his head as if in slow-motion and brushed his mouth over hers. What had begun as a mere touching of lips changed when he deepened the kiss, and if he hadn't been holding her, Natalia doubted whether her knees would've supported her body. Going on tiptoe, she pressed her breasts to his chest and returned the kiss with all of the passion she had been holding in check even months before her breakup.

Hot, angry tears pricked the backs of her eyelids as she struggled not to cry for remaining in a relationship that had long passed its expiration date. It had taken her a while to realize Daryl was responsible for what had become a toxic liaison. When she'd been introduced to the brilliant up-and-coming attorney who had grown up in a depressed area of North Philly, Natalia believed she'd met her soul mate, a man who was just as ambitious as she was. She had become one of the youngest ER supervising physicians at one of Philadelphia's busiest city hospitals while Daryl worked tirelessly to become partner. She'd tried to console him and caution him to be patient but patience wasn't one of his positive personality traits.

"You don't know how long I've wanted to kiss you," Seth whispered against her parted lips.

His query shattered her tortured musings, and Natalia blinked back unshed tears. "And you don't know how long I've *needed* someone to kiss me."

Seth's hands moved up and cradled her face. "Why did you leave Philadelphia?"

"That's a long story," she said, repeating what she'd told Mya Wainwright.

He kissed her again, this time over each eyelid. "I'm not going anywhere and neither are you, so I'm all ears if you need to talk."

Natalia exhaled an inaudible breath. Not only did she need to talk, but to someone she hoped wouldn't judge her. "I needed a new beginning. I was facing impending burnout at the hospital working double and triple shifts, while my personal life was in the toilet but I refused to acknowledge it until it was too late."

Bending slightly, Seth picked Natalia up in his arms and carried her over to the sofa and settled her on the cushion. He returned to the kitchen for the wineglasses and set them on the glass-topped coffee table. Dropping an arm over her shoulders, he pulled Natalia close to his side.

"Talk to me, babe."

"I met Daryl Owens for the first time at a hospital fundraising event." Natalia felt a return of inner strength when she told Seth everything about her relationship with Daryl. They'd dated for two years before he talked about getting married. A cold shiver eddied over her body when she told Seth that Daryl had suggested if he sold his condo and moved in with her, he would have the funds he needed to make partner.

Easing back, Seth stared down at her. "Are you saying he used you?"

She nodded. "Big-time. But I'd believed myself so in love with him that I would've agreed to anything. The following year we officially announced our engagement and he bought me a four-carat marquise diamond ring that overpowered my hand. I couldn't wear it when working at the hospital, so it became a showpiece for whenever we attended social events together. Daryl's mantra was the bigger the better."

Seth shook his head. "Talk about overcompensating."

"Tell me about it," she agreed. Natalia continued, telling him about the city cutting the budgets of some of the municipal hospitals, which left them short-staffed. "There was talk of closing some of the facilities and ours was one on the list. Doctors and nurses were leaving in droves and that left us with a dearth of personnel to treat an underserved population that used the ER as their clinic. I became head supervisor by default and there were weeks when I spent more days sleeping in the doctor's lounge than I did in my own bed.

"Even though we were living together Daryl and I were like two strangers. He complained constantly not because I was working too much, but because I couldn't accompany him to a number of social events. One argument followed with another until it was a tsunami where we couldn't agree on anything. It ended when I came home after working eighteen straight hours to discover he'd moved out, taking the ring and the dog he'd given me for my birthday. I didn't give two hoots about the ring but his taking Oreo left me depressed for weeks. I left him a number of text messages asking that he bring him back, but he didn't reply."

"What a piece of crap," Seth spat out.

"I called him a lot worse than that. But in the end I realized he'd done me a favor because he was out of my life, and it gave me the opportunity to fulfill my dream to become a small-town doctor like my father."

"Doesn't your father have a practice in Philadelphia?"

"No. Daddy set up his practice in Paoli."

"Why in Paoli?"

"That's where I grew up."

"I was under the impression that you were a big-city girl," Seth said.

"Not quite. Paoli is about twenty-five miles from Philly and has a population of about fifty-five hundred people. So, that makes me a small-town girl."

Seth ruffled her short hair. "Does this mean you're seriously thinking about putting down roots here?"

"Only time will tell," Natalia said cryptically. "I enjoy working with Dr. Franklin and I've made a new friend with Mya Wainwright. She invited me to join her and her husband at their table for the Memorial Day picnic."

"I guess we'll be seated together because Giles and I've agreed to share the same table."

She tilted her chin to look up at him. "Do you plan to march in the parade?"

"Yes. Only because the parade begins at eleven and everyone starts gathering on the church lawn at noon for the picnic. Remember, my shift begins at two." Seth dropped his arm and leaned over to pick up Natalia's glass, and then his. "Let's toast to a new beginning."

She touched her glass to his. Talking to Seth about her past relationship had irrevocably changed her; her past was now truly the past. "Here's to new beginnings."

Attractive lines fanned out around Seth's eyes when he stared at her over the rim of his glass. "The worst is behind you, Natalia."

"I know that now." She took a deep swallow of wine as she settled against Seth's chest.

* * *

Seth rested his chin on the top of Natalia's head. She had endured a tumultuous relationship with her ex and fortunately had gotten out before she married him. However, he hadn't been as fortunate.

"You were lucky you didn't marry the clown or he could've made your life a living hell if or when you decided to divorce him."

Natalia stirred slightly. "Is that what happened to you?"

"No. When my wife told me she wanted a divorce because she was carrying another man's child and that he wanted to marry her before the baby was born, we flew to the Dominican Republic for a quickie divorce." Seth felt Natalia stiffen.

"Were you certain it wasn't your child she was carrying?"

"I was very certain. I was stationed overseas for six months and when I returned she was three months pregnant. I accepted some of the blame because I was away for extended periods of time, but I also blame her for never telling me she had a fear of being alone."

"You didn't know this before you married her?"

"No. When I met her she was living with her sister's family. I knew her father had abandoned his family when she and her sister were very young, and that her mother had to move in with their grandmother to make ends meet. Melissa was still in high school when her mother was murdered during an attempted carjacking. Her sister, who was three years older, married her boyfriend and Melissa moved in with them."

"Oh, how sad, Seth."

He nodded. "She'd lost her father, mother and

grandmother before her twenty-first birthday. I knew this when I married her, and it had to be some perverted sense of machismo that made me want to take care of her. She'd been through enough and that's why I agreed to the quickie divorce because things could've gotten messy because she was having an affair with one of my superior officers."

A soft gasp escaped Natalia. "What a lowlife. Couldn't you have reported him?"

"Yes, but it probably would've ruined his career. There are legal issues surrounding fraternization in the military. After the divorce, I put in a request for another overseas post. There was talk about shipping me back to Afghanistan to help train the local police, but I was finally assigned to a base in Okinawa, Japan."

"Lucky you. Did you get to see a lot of the world while you were in the military?"

"Not as much as I should have. Whenever I had leave I'd come home and help my father on whatever job he was working on. Dad was a hard taskmaster and anyone that worked for him knew he was no-nonsense. Once he decided to finish the basement, it took him less than a day to frame the entire space."

"How long did it take him to renovate this house?"

"Almost a year, but that's only because he did it by himself. However, he did wait for me to come home on leave to help him install the granite countertops. The slabs are too heavy for one person to lift."

"Hard taskmaster or not, the man was definitely a perfectionist."

Seth dropped a kiss on her hair. "Dad would've loved hearing you say that."

Natalia untangled her arms. "I hate to be a party pooper, but I need to get up and boil the potatoes."

She pushed off the sofa and Seth felt her loss immediately. Although he'd planned to take Natalia to an upscale restaurant, the weather had forced them to stay inside to share a domesticity he hadn't experienced in years. As newlyweds he and Melissa had moved into a one-bedroom apartment near the base in San Diego, and he'd always looked forward to coming home to his wife who wanted to surprise him with a new dish. Although her cooking skills needed much improvement, Seth always complimented her attempts.

Talking to Natalia about his former wife had conjured up happy times and the shock to discover she had been sleeping with another man. His emotions had run the gamut from rage to anguish that he had failed his wife, that he ignored the signs each time he'd returned that she was different. He'd told Natalia the worst was behind her, and so it was with him.

Seth removed the platter with the steaks and lobster tails from the refrigerator to bring them to room temperature, and then joined Natalia at the cooking island. "I need to see how you're going to make these royal potatoes."

She'd dried and chopped four medium potatoes and placed them in a large pot of boiling water. "After they're tender, I'll drain and mash them and add three egg yolks, a couple tablespoons of cream and grated cheese. After mixing everything thoroughly, I'll pipe the mixture into swirls onto a greased baking sheet. After baking for twenty minutes in a four hundred and twenty-five degree oven until they're golden-brown,

I'll sprinkle them with paprika and voilà! You'll have duchess potatoes."

Seth rested his elbows on the countertop. "It sounds easy enough except for the piping."

"When I get to that stage I'll show you how it's done. I should get at least a dozen potatoes from this recipe and I've made extra slaw for you to have left-overs."

He lifted his eyebrows questioningly. "You don't want to take some home?"

"No. I cook every night and I always make enough for several meals, and that includes lunch."

"Have you eaten lunch at Ruthie's?"

Natalia shook her head. "Not yet. It's going to take a while before I realize I can leave the office for an hour and not come back to a crisis. Working in the ER was akin to running on a treadmill where there's no cutoff switch." She paused. "How long did it take you to transition from military police to a civilian deputy sheriff?"

"Now that I look back, it probably took a year," Seth admitted. "Folks were calling me 'the badass,' which definitely wasn't complimentary. That's when I had to soften my stance and view the people I'd grown up with as neighbors and not potential lawbreakers."

"What was your rank in the Corps?"

"Master sergeant."

Natalia bit back a smile. "Folks were right. You were a badass."

"Why would you say that?" he asked.

"Because all sergeants are badasses. I saw a doc-umentary about marine recruits at Parris Island and the drill sergeant was one scary dude."

"That scary dude is responsible for turning boys and girls into men and women. And once they graduate basic training they know without a doubt they are the military's elite."

Natalia tested the tenderness of the potatoes with a fork. "Life to me is a series of adaptations. We adapt to adulthood and all of the responsibilities that go with it. And we're forced to accept and adjust to the unforeseen events that change who we are and how we view the world around us."

"I've had two years to adjust to life as a civilian, while it shouldn't take you that long to get used to living in a small town again."

"Hopefully it won't take a year because I have to look for a permanent residence before Chandler Evans returns to the States."

Seth sobered. "I'm going to miss having you as a neighbor because not only are you prettier, but you're also a lot friendlier than Chandler."

"Are you saying he's antisocial?"

"No. It's just that he keeps to himself, and that's not easy to do around here because there are very few secrets in The Falls."

A mysterious smile tilted the corners of Natalia's mouth. "Like us going in and out of each other's homes?"

Seth leaned closer. "That, too."

"What do you mean by 'that, too'?"

"Remember folks saw us together at the Wolf Den."

Natalia's jaw dropped. "You mean to say my eating in public with you was cause for gossip?"

"Yep. Number one, I've never taken a woman to the Den as deputy sheriff, and number two, you're the first woman since my mother moved to Georgia that I've invited over. And once we're seated together at the picnic it will be all she wrote for wagging tongues." Seth ran a finger down the length of her nose. "Do you think you're going to be able to deal with the gossip about the deputy sheriff and his lady doctor?"

Natalia rolled her eyes upward. "Please, Seth. Let folks talk. I'm a big girl and I've never been bothered by gossip."

Seth was momentarily speechless by Natalia's pronouncement that she wasn't bothered if they were seen together. He'd remembered her saying she'd just gotten rid of a boyfriend and wasn't looking for another. And, while he hadn't been actively looking for a girlfriend, he found himself more than open to dating Natalia.

"I can't promise you—"

Natalia placed a finger over Seth's mouth and interrupted him. "I don't want you to promise me anything except a modicum of normalcy. My high school boyfriend was a stalker, and the man I dated in college cheated on me. And you know about Daryl who felt it was his right to control my life. He was my third strike, and I swore after him I'd never date again. But if you turn out to be any of the above, then please let me know now before we're seen in public together again."

Seth's fingers curved around her wrist and he kissed the back of her hand. His gaze lowered as did his voice when he said, "I can reassure you that I am none of the above."

"Only time will tell, won't it?"

"I know it's not easy for you to trust a man after what you've gone through with your exes, but there comes a time when you have to let it go."

Natalia's hands stilled. "Have you let it go, Seth? Have you gotten over your wife carrying another man's baby?"

Natalia was asking Seth a question he'd asked himself a number of times over the years. That he had rid himself of the anger and distrust the instant their flight from the Dominican Republic touched down in Miami. He'd left the country married to a woman who'd given another man what should have been his, and when he returned, it was as a single man who knew it would take time to trust another woman again.

"Yes, I have," Seth said truthfully. Even if he hadn't forgiven Melissa.

"Good for you."

"What about you, Natalia?" he asked.

"What about me, Seth?"

"Do you lump all men into the same category as your three strikes?"

Frowning, she shook her head. "Of course not. Not all men are stalkers, cheaters or want submissive women."

And not all women cheat on their husbands, Seth thought. A satisfied light brightened his eyes. He'd just met Natalia, hadn't spent much time with her, yet he was looking forward to their fishing and hiking together.

Chapter Eight

When Natalia parked in her assigned space and walked around to Main Street, she found a crowd standing three-deep along the parade route. So much for her arriving early. Many elderly residents were seated in folding chairs on the sidewalk, while young kids sandwiched in between them on the curb.

Dozens of U.S. flags and red, white and blue bunting hung from lampposts and storefronts. Most of the businesses had closed down for the holiday to give their employees time to be with their families, while it was a picture-perfect day for a parade. There were only a few puffy white clouds in the startlingly blue sky and temperatures were predicted to go as high as seventy-six. Everywhere she went Natalia overheard people talking about the upcoming parade and the following picnic, which they compared to a gigantic tailgate party.

Seth informed her that the Wolf Den and Ruthie's provided the food, which was offset by donations from townspeople. All collected proceeds went directly to the church's outreach for needy families. Someone from the Chamber of Commerce had come to the medical office soliciting donations for the event. The next day Natalia wrote a generous check and dropped it off at the chamber office; the single act bolstered her resolve to become a permanent resident of the town.

She looked forward to going into the medical office where she'd developed a positive working relationship with the staff. She was able to spend more time with her patients than she had with those who'd come into the ER's Trauma Center, and actually gained their trust. Natalia had counseled several women who were overweight while cautioning them about the severity of their condition, which could lead to more serious medical problems. She referred them to Leah who gave them a printout of a diet they should follow and a date for them to return to the office to monitor their progress.

The medical assistant approached her one morning to ask if she could set up a group to counsel patients with nutritional issues. Leah admitted that she'd always had a problem with her weight until she was diagnosed as pre-diabetic. Because her mother and grandmother died from complications from diabetes, it was a wake-up call for her to change her diet and lifestyle. Natalia told her that she would have to discuss it with Dr. Franklin before she could make a decision.

She went on tiptoe in an attempt to see over the

shoulder of a man when she heard the sound of music in the distance. Natalia managed to duck under the arm of a teenage boy until she could view the lead car in the parade with the mayor and his wife sitting in the back seat of the vintage convertible. A pickup with a loudspeaker blaring patriotic songs was filled with the members of the town council. A band from the middle school followed as Boy Scouts, Girl Scouts and Brownies with their troop leaders kept step with the music. Reaching into the pocket of her jeans, Natalia took out her phone to videotape the event as many along the parade route were doing.

It appeared as if every business and civic organization was well represented as their members marched along Main Street wearing sashes identifying themselves. A roar went up from the crowd when the high school's drum and bugle troop demonstrated their skills, which had earned them a number of county and state awards. The fire department was represented with a truck from the late nineteenth century hitched to a pickup. It was followed by a gleaming modern pumper with several volunteer firefighters wearing red suspenders riding on top of it.

The roar of the crowd was deafening when present and former military wearing green, blue and desert fatigues pushed wheelchairs with veterans of foreign wars who'd fought and risked their lives fighting in Europe, the Philippines, Korea and Vietnam. Natalia couldn't take her eyes off Seth in his sand-colored fatigues as he leaned over to listen to something an elderly man wearing a blouse filled with medals was saying to him.

Natalia turned around when she heard a woman

call her name and then pushed her way through a group of several young boys to where Mya Wainwright stood holding Lily. Mother and daughter wore matching baseball caps and sunglasses. Mya's face bore the evidence of her spending time in the tropical sun.

"How long have you been here?" she asked Mya.

"I just arrived. I couldn't find a space and I had to park over near the church and walk. Lily didn't want me to pick her up, so it took what seemed like forever."

"If I'd known you needed a ride I would've picked you up," Natalia said, "because I have a designated spot in back of the office."

Mya blew out her cheeks. "Maybe next year. But I did get a chance to see Giles and Seth when they went by."

"Do you think we can make it to the veterans' monument in time to see the wreath-laying ceremony?" Natalia asked.

"What time is it?" Mya questioned.

Natalia glanced at the time on her phone. "Eleven fifty."

"I doubt it. It's four blocks away and we'll never make it there in time with this crowd. I grew up here and the only thing that brings folks out in droves is this parade and the Fourth of July fair that runs for three days and nights."

"I'll drive you back over to the church. I don't have a car seat for Lily, so you're going to have to sit in the back with her on your lap."

Mya smiled. "Thanks."

* * *

Natalia parked her SUV next to Mya's Honda Odyssey in the church's expansive lot. She removed her baseball cap, reached into her tote and took out a wide-tooth comb to fluff up the short strands. Mouth-watering aromas wafted from an enormous white tent erected several hundred feet away in a grassy area. She got out and opened the rear door and extended her arms to take Lily from Mya. Mother and daughter had also taken off their caps and sunglasses. The toddler hesitated, and then held out her arms to be picked up.

Lily stared at her with large, round blue eyes. "You remember me, don't you?" Natalia asked.

"It's going to take her a while to warm up to you," Mya said, "and when she does, be prepared because she'll ask you a lot of questions."

"That because she's very bright. Right, boo-boo?"

"I no boo-boo," Lily said.

Natalia pretended to be shocked. "If you're not boo-boo, then who are you?"

"Lily!"

"I guess she told me," Natalia said under her breath as she and Mya entered the tent. Rows of tables and benches were set up theater-style, serving tables positioned around the perimeter of the tent, and servers, dressed entirely in white from caps to running shoes, were setting pitchers of water and soft drinks and stacks of plastic cups and napkin-wrapped cutlery on each table.

"This tent reminds me of a revival meeting."

"That's because at one time there were quite a few revivals in The Falls. Every summer different evangelists would come to town. Folks would travel far and wide to listen to their fire and brimstone sermons, and a few claimed to have been healed after they laid hands on them."

Natalia set Lily on her feet when she wiggled to get down. "Do you believe they were healed?"

"I don't know," Mya said, as she led the way to a table with a centerpiece of a small American flag. "I was too young to understand what all of the shouting was all about. My mother was a devoted Southern Baptist and every year she would take me and my sister with her to what she called tent meetings. Despite the music, preaching, crying and shouting I'd fall asleep because it would go on for hours."

The one time her paternal grandmother wanted to take Natalia to a tent meeting, her father forbade it because of his belief that the faith healers were con artists intent on selling salvation to those gullible enough to hand over their hard-earned money.

"Where do you want to sit?" she asked Mya.

"Here is good." She had selected a table near a wide aisle for easy access to and from the food stations. "Traditionally the members of the military are served first. I always have Giles bring me a plate so I don't have to stand in line with the other folks."

Natalia sat down and set her tote on the bench next to her. Mya mentioning food was a reminder that she'd gotten up early to prepare a scant breakfast of toast and coffee before she put up several loads of laundry and cleaned the kitchen and bathroom.

After sharing their surf and turf dinner, she and Seth hadn't had an opportunity to eat together again. A week later he called to tell her he had to work his days off because the sheriff's department was down one man because a deputy was on bereavement leave. When she least expected it, Natalia found herself comparing her relationship with Seth to what she'd initially had with Daryl.

She knew Seth was attracted to her as she was to him, but unlike Daryl, at no time had he put pressure on her to go beyond what she deemed an easygoing friendship. Within half an hour of meeting Daryl, he'd asked if he could take her to dinner to get to know her better. She'd graduated, completed an internship and residency without dating, because she had a hard-and-fast rule not to engage in a workplace romance. What had begun as friendship segued into a physical relationship and an engagement. And it wasn't until after their breakup had she become aware of how ingeniously he had been insinuating himself into her life. The responsibility of supervising the Trauma Center and the long hours spent working at the hospital left her little time to analyze her private life, which had been spiraling out of control. However, she tried to right it when she began to challenge him. Disagreements escalated into shouting matches until she told him either they go to couples counseling or break up. Daryl refused counseling and promised to change. He didn't change and initiated the breakup.

The tent was quickly filling up as residents scrambled to find tables for family members. Natalia estimated there was enough room to seat at least six hundred. "Will everyone in town turn out to eat?" she asked Mya.

"Most of them do. But not everyone comes this early."

"Daddy!" Lily screamed, holding out her arms.

Natalia turned to see a tall, deeply tanned, raven-haired man with Seth heading in their direction. Giles scooped his daughter off Mya's lap and rubbed noses with Lily. Natalia's suspicions that Lily looked like her father was evident when she met the man's laser-blue eyes.

Seth rested a hand on Natalia's shoulder. "Giles, I'd like you to meet Dr. Natalia Hawkins. Natalia, Giles Wainwright."

Leaning over the table, Giles offered her his hand. "It's pleasure meeting you, Dr. Hawkins. Mya has been talking my ear off about inviting you over to welcome you properly to The Falls. Three weeks from now we have family coming down from New York to spend some time with us, so the more the merrier."

She smiled at the drop-dead handsome man with captain bars on his desert fatigues. "Please call me Natalia. I'm only Dr. Hawkins at the office. And I accept your invitation to get together with you and your family."

Giles sat down next to Mya. "Satisfied, sweetheart?"

Mya blew her husband an air-kiss. "Yes, sweetheart." She turned to Seth. "You have to let us know when you're off because you know you're always welcome to join us."

Seth sat next to Natalia and dropped an arm over her shoulders. "I'm off Saturdays, barring any unforeseen schedule changes." He pressed a kiss to her cheek. "Is that your Saturday to work, babe?"

Natalia felt a rush of heat creep up her chest to her face. Seth's endearment had slipped out so smoothly as if it was something he'd always called her. "Yes, but I'm off at one."

Mya waved a hand. "That works because we usually start cooking around three." She flashed a Cheshire cat grin. "I guess that settles it."

Seth's hand moved from her shoulders and down the length of her spine. "Did you get to see the parade?"

She met his smiling light brown eyes. "Yes. It's nice to see that the armed forces are well represented in The Falls."

Seth laughed softly. "Now you sound like a local. Folks around here hardly ever say Wickham Falls when they're talking about The Falls."

"I'd like to think of myself as a local. After all, I do live here."

"If you say so."

Natalia gave Seth an incredulous look. There was something in his rejoinder that caused a cold chill to eddy over her body. "Why would you say that?"

"Say what?"

"What you just said. Don't you believe me when I say that I plan to stay here?"

"What I believe or want should not affect your decision to stay or leave The Falls, Natalia," he said in a quiet voice. "And there is one thing I want you to remember, and that is I'm not your ex. I will never tell you what you should or should not do."

Natalia closed her eyes and smiled. "You could never be him," she said, after she opened her eyes. There was so much about him she liked and missed: his warmth, the now-familiar scent of his cologne and his soft, drawling voice with a trace of a Southern accent.

A server approached their table. "Captain Wainwright and Sergeant Collier, you can go up and get your food now."

Seth stood. "What do you want, babe?"

"Bring me whatever you think I'd like."

He nodded. "Okay."

Seth followed Giles as they walked to the food stations. He had less than two hours to spend with Natalia and his friends before he was scheduled to start his shift. He was a first responder and that meant working weekends and holidays.

"You're right, Collier," Giles said as he picked up two Styrofoam plates.

"What about?"

"Natalia. She's stunning and a doctor."

When Giles mentioned that Mya had talked nonstop about the young woman doctor who'd joined Dr. Franklin's practice, Seth told him that Natalia was his neighbor and admitted that she was beautiful and brainy.

"I like her."

"No!" Giles said, smiling. "Only a blind man wouldn't be able to see that, Brother Collier."

Seth picked up two plates. "I'll have some potato salad," he said to the server. "At least I'm man enough to admit it, Brother Wainwright," he said, lowering his voice. "The only drawback is that we don't get to see that much of each other with our work schedules."

Giles pointed to a tray of baked beans. "It was that way when I first met Mya. My schedule had me flying between here, New York and the Bahamas at least three or four times a month. And then when I'd schedule a time to take them with me, Lily would come down with an ear infection or a cold and all our plans would go up in smoke. It wasn't until we were married and I told a cousin that Mya and I were planning to have a baby together that he agreed to join the company's international division."

"You're telling me this to say what?"

"Be patient. Things have a way of working themselves out."

Seth wanted to tell his fellow marine that at thirty-eight, he was quickly running out of patience. He'd been with enough women following his divorce to recognize that after a month Natalia was different, that she possessed all of the attributes he wanted in a wife.

He'd been twenty-seven and Melissa twenty-two when they married and at that time he'd believed he was mature enough to be a husband and father. They'd talked about starting a family but Melissa wanted to wait until he returned from his deployment. She feared if he was killed that her child would grow up without a father like she did.

It had taken ten years for him to get over his distrust of all women. Even when making love he forced himself to remain detached from the most intimate act between a man and a woman. He'd thought of it as a physical release and nothing beyond that.

This was not to say he didn't want to sleep with Natalia but that wasn't a priority for him. Seth enjoyed them talking, cooking and just sitting together listening to music. Her presence offered him a peace he hadn't known possible. And because he was aware that she had been unlucky in love he knew he had to let her take the lead in whatever relationship he hoped to have with her.

"You're probably right," he said after a comfortable pause.

"I know I'm right, Seth. We both were blindsided. The difference is the woman I occasionally saw had my baby and I didn't find out about it until after she passed away. I was luckier than you because Lily was actually my daughter. But I must say you're a hell of a good guy—you could've punished your ex by not agreeing to the divorce and raising the child as your own. And then there's the other side when you could've reported your superior officer for sleeping with your wife."

"I don't like a mess, Giles."

"Neither do I. Most times I agree with Mya rather than argue about what turns out to be nothing more than minutia."

A hint of a smile parted Seth's lips. "Being deployed makes you look at life differently because you don't know whether your next breath will be your last."

"Amen, brother," Giles whispered.

They moved along the food line selecting from an assortment of hot and cold dishes until reaching the meat station. He touched elbows with the Wolf Den's pit master extraordinaire Aiden Gibson. The tall, blond, former Navy SEAL had affixed the trident pin to his blouse. Most folks in The Falls weren't aware that Aiden had been a SEAL until he married his daughters' teacher in a military ceremony last fall.

"How's the family?"

Aiden smiled. "All is good in the Gibson hood," he quipped.

"Are they here?"

"My girls are coming with my sister. Taryn's staying home because she's too close to her due date."

"Have you guys picked out a name for your son?"

The skin around Aiden's bluish-green eyes fanned out when he smiled. "We went back and forth and finally settled on Daniel Marcus Gibson."

Seth nodded. "That's a nice strong name for a boy."

"Speaking of babies. There must be something in the water because Sawyer Middleton just told me he and Jessica are expecting their first baby before the end of the year. And there's also something calling folks to come back to The Falls. You came back and so did Sawyer, and I overheard talk at the Den that Leland Remington is moving back to help his sister run the boardinghouse."

"How many years has it been since Lee left?"

"Too many to count," Aiden said.

Seth heard someone clear their throat behind him. "I'm standing here jawing and holding up the line." He extended the empty plate. "I'll have some pulled pork, fried chicken, brisket and ribs." Aiden filled the plate with meat from the trays under the heat lamps. "Thanks, Chief Petty Officer Gibson."

Aiden gave Seth a snappy salute. "My pleasure, Master Sergeant Collier."

Seth returned to the table and set the plates down in front of Natalia. "I got a little bit of this and that."

She pressed her shoulder to his. "Everything looks delicious. I'm going to get some empty plates so we can all share."

"Don't get up," Giles said. He handed Lily to Mya. "I'll get them."

Seth rested his hand at the small of Natalia's back. Giles was right. He had to be patient and let their friendship and hopefully a relationship unfold naturally. He'd promised Natalia that he wouldn't stalk, cheat or attempt to control her life, and if he broke any of those promises he knew whatever he hoped to share with her was doomed.

He thought about what Aiden said about their peers returning to The Falls. He, like many others he'd attended school with, felt their existence too insular, the town too cloistered and they wanted a change.

Sawyer enlisted in the military, founded a New York–based software company and came back a multimillionaire.

Giles had joined Sawyer as the newest multimillionaire when the real estate mogul married Mya and made Wickham Falls his permanent home.

Talk that Lee Remington was planning to return was certain to divide the townsfolk who either loved or hated Leland. Some were quick to judge the young man who'd insisted he was innocent, and even after he had been exonerated they contained to blame him.

Seth went completely still when Natalia rested a hand on his thigh under the table. He stared across the table at Lily as Mya fed her a spoonful of mac and cheese in an attempt not to concentrate on how close her fingers were to his groin. "What are you doing?" he asked between clenched teeth.

Natalia removed her hand. The lashes that shadowed her cheeks flew up. "What's the matter?"

He saw indecision in her eyes and chided himself

for overreacting. It was apparent she wasn't attempting to seduce him. "I'm sorry. I was thinking about something else," Seth lied smoothly, something he loathed doing to her.

Reaching for the pitcher of water, he filled a cup and took a deep swallow. The icy liquid cooled his chest but did little to quench the fire between his thighs.

Chapter Nine

"Drs. Franklin and Hawkins, you're needed in the waiting room!"

A week following the Memorial Day celebration Natalia rushed out of her office where she'd updated a patient's chart to see why Angela had summoned her and Henry to the front of the office. Henry was several steps behind her, and jolt of adrenaline kicked in when she saw Seth lowering his boss to the floor. Roger Jensen's face was flushed and the front of his khaki uniform was stained from the blood streaming from his nose.

"I need gloves," she shouted. Within seconds a pair of disposable gloves appeared and she slipped them on. "What happened?" she asked Seth as he knelt beside her.

"He said he was feeling dizzy and was going to

lie down for a while. When he began complaining of a headache followed by a nosebleed, I knew it was time he see a doctor."

Henry took over while Natalia checked the lawman's vitals. "I need everyone to clear the office. Please step outside," he ordered when several people began complaining about not wanting to wait.

Natalia saw concern in Seth's eyes. "He needs to go to the hospital. He's in hypertensive crisis. His blood pressure is one-eighty over one-twenty."

Seth activated the radio attached to his shoulder and spoke quietly and calmly into it. "The EMTs are on their way. Aren't you going to give him something?"

She rested a hand on his shoulder. "No. The EMTs will stabilize him before he gets to the hospital." The words were barely off her tongue when two men came in with a gurney. Natalia gave them her findings as they placed Roger onto the rolling stretcher and strapped him in.

Lines of tension ringed Seth's mouth as he forced a smile. "Thank you. I'm going to ride with them. I'll call your cell to update you on his condition."

Natalia nodded. "Okay."

"You handled that nicely," Henry said when the door closed behind Seth and the technicians. "It looks as if you haven't lost your touch when it comes to a crisis."

She took off the gloves and discarded them in a container for infectious materials. "I've seen enough medical emergencies to last a couple of lifetimes."

Henry pushed his hands into the pockets of his

white coat. "The last time I saw Roger I told him he had to exercise and lose at least fifty pounds."

"Let's hope he'll take your advice after this scare."

"Angela, you can let the people in now," he told the receptionist.

Angela walked to the door and opened it. "You can come in now."

Seth lost track of time as he waited for Roger to be evaluated in the county's medical center. He'd opted to remain at the hospital rather than return to The Falls with the technicians. He called Michelle, the sheriff's wife, to reassure her that he would stay with Roger until she arrived.

Georgina had called him twice to check on Roger's condition. And he repeated to her what he'd told Roger's wife, that the doctors wouldn't tell him anything about the sheriff's condition until Michelle got there. Georgina told him Andy had volunteered to cover his shift and that he would run the department as assistant sheriff until Roger's return. Seth thought Andy was being premature about taking over the department when Roger was still officially responsible.

His cell phone vibrated again and he glanced at the screen. Natalia was calling him. Seth left the waiting room for an area where he would be able to use the phone. "Hey, babe."

"How is he?"

"I don't know yet. They're still running tests. Roger's wife is on her way."

"I'm coming to the hospital."

He heard a signal indicating she'd ended the call. Seth knew it would take Natalia at least twenty minutes to get to the hospital, which gave him enough time to get coffee from the snack bar before it closed for the night.

Seth garnered curious stares when he walked into the renovated snack bar that reminded him of those in airport terminals. The hospital had been in disrepair before the board began an aggressive fund-raising campaign to renovate the facility and install the latest medical equipment.

The clerk at the register offered him a friendly smile. "Good evening, Deputy. That coffee has been there awhile, so if you're willing to wait I'll put on a fresh pot."

The liquid in the half-filled pot resembled sludge. Seth returned her smile and nodded.

He thumbed through a magazine while he waited for the clerk to brew the coffee. The distinctive aroma wafted to his nose. He filled a large container, added a splash of creamer and handed the clerk a bill.

"Keep the change."

"But…but you gave me too much."

"No, I didn't. The tip is for the fresh coffee."

"Thank you," she called out to his retreating back.

"You're welcome."

Seth sat in the same chair he'd vacated earlier to await word on Roger's condition. Stretching out his legs, he crossed his booted feet at the ankles. The plastic chair was uncomfortable and not constructed for someone wearing a gun belt. He'd drunk half the coffee when Natalia walked into the waiting area. She hadn't bothered to change out of her scrubs and had the leather tote she seemed to bring everywhere with her.

Pushing to his feet, he went over to her. "How fast did you drive to get here?"

"I did exceed the speed limit by a few miles." Natalia touched his hand. "Stay here. I'm going to use a little professional clout to check on Roger's condition."

He watched as she walked over to the nurses' station and spoke quietly to the woman wearing a floral pink tunic. Minutes later a young doctor appeared and spoke with Natalia. Seth couldn't pull his gaze away from her. She and the doctor were similarly dressed and in that instant her choice of a profession was even more evident. When she'd asked to look at his injured thumb and revealed she was a doctor, it hadn't actually registered with him.

But when he watched her take charge to check Roger's blood pressure, monitor his heartbeat and examine his eyes while at the same time comforting him with words that had put Roger at ease made him realize becoming a doctor had been Natalia's calling. He had half supported and half carried Roger from the station house to the medical office, fearing the worst when his nose began bleeding. Seth was certain his boss was having a heart attack or a stroke. The technicians had stabilized him during the ride to the hospital where the staff met them upon their arrival.

Natalia approached Seth, and took his hand. "The doctor says they're going to keep Roger for a few days because they want to monitor his blood pressure. They ran a CT scan and the results show he suffered a small stroke. They also had to cauterize his nose to stop the bleeding."

Seth froze. "A stroke?" he repeated.

"A very mild stroke, Seth. Right now he's resting."

"Can we see him?"

"The doctor said we could, but only for a few minutes. His wife is with him right now. Come with me. He's in room two-fifteen." Natalia knew Seth was concerned about his boss's condition, but Roger was in the best place where he could be closely monitored. They followed the signs to the elevator and took the car to the second floor. "This is a nice hospital."

"Do you miss working in a hospital?"

She gave him a sidelong glance. "No. Been there, done that." Natalia sanitized her hands from the dispenser outside Roger's room before entering. He was hooked up to an IV and a machine monitoring his vitals.

He slowly turned his head. "Hey. I didn't expect to see you two tonight. Michelle just left to go to the snack bar. She has to eat to stabilize her blood sugar."

Natalia walked closer to the bed. The readings on the monitor indicated a decrease in his blood pressure. "I wanted to be certain you're all right."

Roger's eyelids fluttered. "I am now. If Seth hadn't insisted I come down to your office I doubt whether I'd be talking to you right now."

Seth stood at the foot of the bed. "What's the expression? A hard head makes for a soft behind."

Roger chuckled. "No lie. I've been stuck a few times in the behind already." He sobered quickly. "I'm not sure how long I'll be here, and even after I'm released, how long I'll be out of work. Seth, I want you to stand in as acting sheriff until I'm medically cleared to return."

Natalia stared at Seth who appeared shocked by

Roger's suggestion. "What about Andy?" he asked. "He's the next in line to replace you."

"I'm well aware of the department's table of organization, but I have the authority to choose who I want to replace me in case of an emergency. Andy's a good deputy but he's no supervisor. Once Michelle gets back I'm going to use her cell phone to poll the council members and issue an official memo designating you as the acting sheriff of Wickham Falls."

Seth crossed his arms over his chest. "I just wish you would've discussed it with me first."

"I didn't have time," Roger countered. "Besides, I didn't know whether you were here or back in the office. I made my decision and I'm going to stand by it."

"You could've—"

"Please let it go, Seth," Natalia admonished quietly, interrupting him. The man had just suffered a stroke, albeit a mild one, and she didn't want Seth to cause him further anxiety that would increase his blood pressure.

Seth narrowed his eyes at her. "Okay. We'll talk about this when you're feeling better."

Roger shifted to get into a more comfortable position. "Yeah, yeah, yeah. Now, can you two get out of here so I can try to catch a few winks before my wife gets back. Knowing her, she's going to read me the riot act about eating right and exercising."

Natalia adjusted several pillows under his shoulders. "Once you're released, I want you to come into the office so our medical assistant can talk to you about joining a group we've been thinking about starting geared specifically to diets and nutrition."

"I'm not doing yoga."

"You don't have to do yoga. The easiest and cheapest method of exercise is walking. Instead of sitting at your desk all day you should get up and walk around the business district."

"Seth already offered to let me use his exercise equipment, but so far I haven't taken him up on it."

Seth smiled for the first time since Roger mentioned his becoming acting sheriff in his absence. "And the offer still stands."

Roger closed his eyes and Natalia knew that was the signal for them to leave so the man could sleep. She didn't know why the sheriff hadn't taken Seth up on his offer to work out in his home. He had divided a section of the finished basement into an in-home gym with a treadmill, rowing machine and an elliptical bike. Roger was like a few of the patients she'd treated at the clinic. Although aware that they had to change or moderate their lifestyle, it wasn't a priority until it became a crisis.

"How are you getting back to The Falls?" Natalia asked Seth as they made their way to the visitor parking lot.

"Georgina called to say she would pick me up."

"Who's Georgina?"

"She's our clerk."

"Oh, I see."

Seth stopped when they reached the white BMW. "Do you, babe? When you asked who Georgina was, I thought you sounded a little jealous."

Natalia's jaw dropped. "Me? Jealous? I think not." She touched the button on the door handle, unlocking the vehicle. "In fact, I don't have a jealous bone in my body."

"I can truthfully say there's no other woman in my life."

"And if you were interested in another woman it wouldn't matter to me because—" Seth's mouth covered hers, stopping whatever she'd planned to say. The kiss only lasted seconds but left her mouth throbbing and wanting more. Curving her arms around his waist, Natalia buried her face between his neck and shoulder as she waited for her runaway heartbeat to resume a normal rhythm.

"You're protesting too much, darling." Resting his hands on her shoulders, he led her around to the passenger side and assisted her in. "I'll drive back."

Although his kiss had stopped her protests, she could not dismiss the sensations, many she'd long forgotten, whirling within her.

Did she like him?

Yes.

Did she want to spend more time with him?

Yes again.

And she wanted him and needed him more than she had any other man. So did she want to sleep with him? The answer was yes again.

The nights she had sat on her porch listening for the sound of the pickup pulling into the neighboring driveway reminded Natalia of her mother who used to sit up and wait for her to come home at night after she'd gotten her driver's license. And no matter how many times she told her mother she would never drink and drive, her entreaty fell on deaf ears. Sylvia Hawkins said it was her right as a mother to worry about her children.

But Seth wasn't her child. He was her neighbor

and more than capable of taking care of himself. He'd spent eighteen years in the Marines as a military police officer, deployed to Afghanistan and now had returned to his hometown to serve as a deputy sheriff. And for more than half his life he carried a gun on his person.

As Seth headed back to The Falls she recalled the nights he'd come home much later than usual and it suddenly hit her. Natalia was afraid he'd gotten involved in a confrontation where he may have been killed or injured. The images of bodies wheeled into the Trauma Center with gunshot and knife wounds came rushing back like frames of film. The sounds of screams, moans and prayers all merged into a cacophony which added to the chaos as she and the medical staff working tirelessly to save lives.

"Do you always talk to your patients?"

Seth's query shattered her reverie. She stared at his distinctive profile as he drove out of the lot. "Most times. It becomes a distraction. I usually sing nursery rhymes to little kids before I give them a shot."

"Do you rap to teenagers?"

Natalia laughed. "No. Sometimes I talk about sports or fashion or whatever they're interested in."

"That sounds a little unorthodox."

"Don't knock it, Seth, because it works. I once treated a high school football phenom who was brought in with a gunshot wound to his lower back only because he happened to be at the wrong place at the wrong time. He was inconsolable because he feared having to give up his dream to play college ball. I was able to stabilize him before he went into the OR."

Seth gave her a quick glance. "What happened to him?"

"He made a full recovery and went on to become a first-round draft by the Philadelphia Eagles. We've kept in touch and he would send me a couple of tickets to every one of his home games." Tickets Daryl coveted whenever a messenger delivered them to her, and had become a source of contention between them when she gave them to her brother, father and brother-in-law whenever she was scheduled to work.

Seth signaled, then maneuvered smoothly into another lane. "I like the feel of your Beemer."

"You like it better than your Charger?"

"Nah! Your SUV is pretty, but there's nothing better than hearing the roar of a muscle car's engine. Some police departments around the country are using Chargers as cruisers."

Natalia glanced at the clock on the dashboard. It was close to seven thirty. "Are you going back to work?"

Seth shook his head. "No. The assistant sheriff is covering my shift. If you don't mind, I'd like to stop at the Den and have dinner before we go home."

She glanced down at her scrubs. "I don't want to go in wearing these."

"What if I call in an order and pick it up?"

"That'll work." Her cell phone chimed a ringtone.

"Aren't you going to answer your phone?" Seth asked.

"It's a text message. I'll look at it later."

A pregnant pause ensued until Seth asked, "What do you want from the Den?"

"Anything that isn't fried or rare."

Using one hand, Seth unbuttoned the pocket on his uniform blouse and handed Natalia his cell. "Scroll through the directory for the Wolf Den and order what you want."

"What do you want?"

"Whatever the day's special is."

Seth emerged from the restaurant to find Natalia staring straight ahead. She looked as if she'd been carved out of stone. He placed the shopping sack with their food on the floor behind the driver's-side seat, and got in next to her.

He touched her arm. "What's the matter, Natalia?" She handed him her phone. Seth swore under his breath when he stared at the photo of a well-dressed man holding a tiny dark-brown-and-white poodle. The text message read:

Oreo misses you and so do I.

He struggled not to lose his temper. "The clown is trying to mess with your head."

Natalia closed her eyes as tears trickled down her face. "I know that. But…but I miss my dog."

Seth gently rubbed her back in an attempt to comfort her. This was a Natalia he'd never witnessed. He was used to the feisty woman who'd survived a tumultuous relationship with a man who tried to bend her to his will, and she'd survived. She'd admitted to having two other relationships which had ended badly, and still she survived. Dr. Natalia Hawkins was a strong, intelligent, independent woman who'd taken control of her life and sought to change it when she relocated from Philadelphia to a town with two stoplights, but it was obvious her jackass of an ex knew exactly how to push her buttons.

Reaching over, Seth cradled the back of her head. "It's okay, babe. He'll get his."

Natalia sniffled and blotted her face with a crumbled tissue. "I'm sorry I lost it."

He kissed her temple. "You're entitled to lose it, Natalia. You don't have to be a superwoman every day all year. Even superheroes take time off to act like normal people."

Her moist lashes fluttered wildly. "You're a fine one to talk, Johnny Lawman. You're on duty even when you're not working. You try to hide that little automatic either at the small of your back or around your ankle, but I know it's there."

Seth rubbed his nose over her cheekbone. "That's because I'm required to carry it even when off-duty. But once I take off the uniform I'm able to separate myself from deputy sheriff Collier."

Natalia shook her head. "Correction alert. Remember you're now the acting sheriff of Wickham Falls."

He lowered his eyes. "It's still not official."

"But it will be."

The news that Roger had selected Seth to stand in for him rather than Andy would generate a lot of gossip—positive and negative. "Is that what you want? For me to be sheriff?"

Natalia touched the tissue to her nose. "If in the future you were to run for the office you definitely would have my vote."

He started up the engine. "That's not going to happen because I'm not into politics beyond voting."

"Not even if I become your campaign manager?"

"No." Seth pulled out of the restaurant parking lot and drove in the direction of the local road. "We've both had a stressful day. What do you say about spending the night with me? After a good night's sleep, you should feel better in the morning." Seeing her cry had tugged at his heart.

"You want me to sleep with you?"

"Did I say that, Natalia? I invited you to sleep over, not sleep with me."

Natalia stared out the side window. "Are you afraid I'm going to have another meltdown?"

"That's only half of it."

She turned to meet his eyes when he slowed as signs for the railroad crossing came into view. "What's the other half?"

"I don't need to be alone tonight."

"Need or want?" Natalia asked.

"Need, babe. When I picked up Roger after he'd passed out, I had a flashback of carrying a buddy who'd literally been blown apart seconds after he'd attempted to detain a woman who'd detonated her suicide belt."

Natalia placed her hand over his on the steering wheel. "Do you still have flashbacks?"

"Not as many as I used to. The last one before Roger's was when I saw the driver of that minivan bleeding from his head after I forced him off the road."

"I'm so sorry, Seth. And you're right. We don't need to be alone tonight. What's sad is that we've both experienced more than our share of death and dying. I'm going to stop at my place first and get a change of clothes I need for tomorrow, then I'll be over."

Seth felt as if he'd won a small victory to get Natalia to spend the night with him. She needed him and he needed her.

Natalia lingered at her house long enough to shower, change into a pair of lounging pants and oversize T-shirt, and pack an overnight bag with clothes for the next day. Seth had left his door unlocked and when she walked in she found him waiting for her. He'd also showered and had exchanged his uniform for gray sweatpants and a black tank top that revealed the power in his muscled upper body.

He took the bag from her loose grip. "I just put some of the dishes in the oven to reheat."

"It smells wonderful."

Seth set her bag on the floor next to the armchair and steered her into the kitchen. She'd ordered smothered chicken with onions and mushrooms."

When he turned to check on the food in the oven Natalia remembered the colorful tattoo on his right shoulder and the one over his heart from when she'd given him the massage. "How long have you had your tattoos?" she asked.

"I got the Semper Fidelis one a few months after I passed basic training, and the Marine Corps Military Police insignia after graduating military police training. Do you have any ink?"

"No," she said, laughing.

"Why not? Nowadays women have as much ink as men."

"I'm not one of those. And what would I get?"

Seth winked at her as he slipped on an oven mitt.

"What about a caduceus? After all, you are a physician."

Natalia shook her head. "That's not happening because I have an aversion to snakes and I definitely don't want one stamped on my body." She crossed the kitchen and gathered plates and flatware to set the table.

"If you did decide to get one where would you put it?" Seth questioned as he took out a microwavable dish and placed it on a trivet.

"It definitely would be somewhere that's not easily visible."

"That's no fun. Only someone who would see you without your clothes would get to enjoy it."

She gave him a saccharine grin. "Exactly." Natalia set the plates on a place mat. "Do you know what I've noticed?"

"What's that?"

"That we only get together over food."

Seth took another plate from the oven. "That's because our work hours don't coincide like most normal couples."

Her hands stilled. "Are we a couple, Seth?"

He stared at her under lowered lids. "Of course we are. Did you think otherwise?"

Natalia lifted her shoulders. "I wasn't sure."

"You're not sure because we haven't made love with each other?" he asked.

"Sleeping together doesn't necessarily make two people a couple."

There were times when she made love with Daryl she'd felt as if she was just going through the motions because it was something two people who lived together and shared a bed do. And if she had been truly honest with herself Natalia would say his lovemaking never rocked her world as she'd heard her girlfriends talk about their experiences with other men.

Seth came closer and cradled her face in his hands. "No, it doesn't. Some people are couples in bed, but share nothing beyond that. I'm no choirboy when it comes to women. And I'm ashamed to say I've slept with some not because I wanted them but because I needed to release sexual frustration."

Leaning closer, Natalia brushed a kiss over Seth's mouth. She did not want to believe that she was having a mature conversation with a man who wasn't afraid to admit his shortcomings when it came to women. "There's no need to beat up on yourself, Seth—women use men for the same reason. And don't ask me if I've done it because I'll plead the Fifth. The only thing you need to know is that I'm not a virgin."

He smiled. "And the only thing you need to know about me is that I've never slept with a woman without using protection."

"Good for you. If more men used condoms it would lower the number of cases of STDs."

Lowering his head, Seth trailed light kisses along the column of her neck. "Spoken like a true medical professional. Are you certain there's nothing else I need to know about you?"

Natalia moaned deep in her throat when Seth's hot breath seared her ear. "I'm on birth control." She'd stopped taking an oral contraceptive when she and Daryl lived together and had her ob-gyn insert an IUD.

"So, you're not ready to become a momma."

"No. But I'm not saying I don't want children."

"You'd make a wonderful mother."

"How do you know that?" she questioned.

"I saw you with Lily. She couldn't stop laughing when you whispered something in her ear. Whenever I go over to see Giles she just sits there and gives me a death stare, and to this day I don't know what I did for her to look at me like that."

"Maybe she's sizing you up. And you have to remember she's daddy's little girl."

Seth released Natalia and pulled out a chair at the table. "Daddy's and mommy's. Mya was a few years behind me in school which meant she wasn't one of the girls I hung out with. Please sit and I'll serve you."

Natalia sat and smiled up at Seth over her shoulder, wondering how she'd gotten so lucky to meet someone like him. He was the complete opposite of all of the men she'd been involved with and she chided herself for wasting her time with losers whom she'd known early on weren't Mr. Right, but Mr. Right Now. She knew she couldn't get back the years or time but vowed the next man in her life would have to be a certified Mr. Right.

Although she wasn't in love with Seth, Natalia knew it would be so easy to love him. All she had to do was trust him enough to let him into her life.

"As soon as we finish eating I'll make up the bed in the guestroom for you."

"You don't have to do that," she said quietly. "I've seen your bed and it's big enough for two people."

Seth halted spooning a portion of green beans onto his plate. "You want to share my bed?"

Natalia bit back a smile when she saw his shocked

expression. "Yes. We can sleep together without making love."

"Is that want you want, Natalia?"

She nodded. "I do for now."

His expression changed as he flashed a smile she interpreted as triumph. "Okay."

Chapter Ten

"Were you aware that you snore?"

Natalia opened her eyes and exhaled a soft sigh. "No, I don't." She'd gotten into bed before Seth and fell asleep before he joined her.

"How do you know?" he whispered against the nape of her neck.

"Because no one ever told me that I do."

"I take that back. Maybe those were sighs instead of snores."

She turned over and met a pair of light brown eyes that were filled with perpetual laughter. "What happened to good morning?"

Winking, Seth kissed the end of her nose. "Good morning, darling."

Natalia buried her face against the hollow of his throat. "That's better."

"Where's my good morning?"

She rested her hand on his shoulder and, slowly and deliberately, she ran her fingers down his upper arm, over his pectorals, flat belly and even lower to the waistband of a pair of drawstring pajama pants. Her fingertips traced the indentation of his belly button.

"Good morning."

Throwing back his head, Seth laughed loudly. "I like your good morning."

She snuggled closer to his hard, warm body and buried her face between his neck and shoulder. "What time is it?"

"It's a little after six."

Natalia moaned softly. "It's still too early to get up."

"What time do you normally get up in the morning?"

"I try to stay in bed until seven. I know I'll never catch up on all of the hours I lost working around the clock in the ER, but I'm going to try."

Seth ran his fingers through her short hair. "Did you take something to keep you alert?"

"No. Most times I operated on pure adrenaline. But whenever I got the chance to lie down, I was asleep as soon as my head touched the pillow."

"Like last night," Seth teased. "You were out like a light when I came to bed. Do you always wear your hair this short?"

"Why? You don't like it?" Natalia knew she sounded defensive because her short hairstyle had become another point of contention between her and Daryl.

"Did I say I didn't like it?"

"No, but—"

"No buts, Natalia," Seth interrupted. "I only asked because I think the style is perfect for your gorgeous face."

She lowered her eyes demurely. "Thank you."

"Don't thank me, babe. Thank your parents for creating such an incredibly beautiful baby girl that grew up to become a stunning woman."

"You're just full of compliments this morning," she teased.

"You think I'm just blowing smoke, Natalia?" His query was laced with a thread of hardness. "You think I'm lying to you because I have an ulterior motive? Don't compare me to your ex because there's nothing I want from you except trust and honesty. I want you to trust me enough to tell me what you like or don't like. And if I do something that bothers you, then let me know and not stew about it. I'm not perfect, Natalia. And there's times when I'm not the easiest guy to get along with because I believe in not bending the rules. And if there comes a time when you don't want to be with me, then just say the word and I'll walk away with no hard feelings."

"She really did a number on you, didn't she?"

A deep frown settled between his eyes. "Who are you talking about?"

"Your ex-wife, Seth. You talked about going down to the Caribbean for a quickie divorce as if you needed to get away from the hustle and bustle of a big city for a few days. I saw the pain in your eyes when you talked about her carrying another man's baby. A baby that should've been yours. You were hurt and you're still hurting. And I'm willing to bet that you don't trust women, otherwise you would've gotten married again."

Seth closed his eyes and counted slowly to ten. He wanted to tell Natalia not to psychoanalyze him. He'd spent hours talking to doctors to cope with the underlying causes of his divorce without divulging the name of the officer who'd seduced his wife and gotten her pregnant. There were times when he'd wanted revenge, to unburden himself when he confronted the man who had taken advantage of a vulnerable woman. Trust. He'd struggled with it for so long that it had kept him from forming a normal relationship with a woman—until Natalia.

She was the first woman he felt comfortable enough with to say whatever he thought or felt. There wasn't a need to censor himself with her. He had invited her into his home and his bed, and when he woke to find her beside him, it seemed so natural, normal that he wondered what it was that made her different from the other women he'd met. Although he was more than physically attracted to her, he didn't feel an urgent need to make love with her.

"You think you know me that well?" he asked.

Natalia threw her leg over his. "No, because you're not that transparent."

"Then what is it?"

"There are times when you're wound so tight that I can feel your tension. You call me babe and darling and claim we're a couple, and I think you say those things because maybe you think that's what I want to hear." She shifted slightly and splayed a hand over his chest. "I like you, Seth. I like you a lot more than

I want to. I'd told myself I didn't want or need another relationship because I always muck them up."

"Maybe you've been given a second chance where you won't muck it up again."

"We'll have to wait and see, won't we?"

"I don't issue endearments glibly."

"I guess that makes me special," Natalia said teasingly.

Seth smiled. "Yes." He wanted to tell Natalia that she was more than special. That he was developing feelings for her he hadn't felt in a very long time.

"I don't know if you really want to get involved with me because I've always been an overachiever and career-minded."

"I can think of worse traits," Seth countered.

"Speaking of psychological traits it took me a while to acknowledge that I was trying to prove to my father that although he was disappointed that his son didn't follow in his footsteps to become a doctor, I told him I would because that's all I ever wanted to be. And it had nothing to prove that following in his footsteps was just as good as my brother following him. Daddy's proud to boast about another generation of Dr. Hawkins, but he's not too happy that I've refused to join his practice."

"Do you think you'll take it over in the future?"

"No."

"What makes you so certain, Natalia? One of these days you may change your mind and move back home."

"Wickham Falls is my home now. It's a place where I can practice medicine, meet new people and make new friends. I've overheard people talk about leaving

The Falls because there's nothing here for them, but it's different for me. It's become my happy place, and unless something drastic happens I plan to be here for a very long time. I'll have to start looking for a house before Chandler comes back to the States."

Seth kissed her hair. "Thankfully that's not going to be for a while, so I get to have you as my neighbor for the next ten or eleven months."

"I'm going to have to get up, Seth, because nature is calling me."

"What do you want for breakfast?"

Natalia stretched her arms over her head and slipped off the bed. "Surprise me."

Seth crossed his arms over his chest and stared at Natalia's retreating figure in a pair of floral pajama shorts with a matching tank top. He couldn't help smiling when he realized how natural it felt to sleep with her without making love.

The cell phone on the bedside table vibrated and he wondered who was calling him this early. He picked up the phone and noted the caller. "Yes, Mayor Gillespie. I can be there at nine." The call lasted only seconds. The mayor wanted to swear him in as acting sheriff in Roger's absence.

Seth placed his right hand on the Bible and raised his left and swore an oath to uphold the principles and responsibilities as acting sheriff of Wickham Falls to the best of his ability. He'd arrived at the town hall and was escorted into the mayor's office to find the town clerk and photographer on hand to witness his swearing-in.

Seth had attended Tyler Gillespie's swearing-in a

couple of months before when he defeated the long-time incumbent by more than 90 percent of the registered voters to become at thirty-six the youngest mayor in the town's history.

Tyler shook Seth's hand, holding it firmly while the photographer got off several shots. "Congratulations, Sheriff Collier."

Seth smiled at the slender man with large green eyes and thick wavy auburn hair falling over his forehead who appeared no older than a college student. He'd started a campaign on a shoestring budget and soundly trounced the former mayor who was so confident that he would be reelected that he hadn't bothered to solicit votes.

"Thank you, Mayor."

Tyler waved to the clerk and the photographer. "Excuse me, gentlemen, I need to talk to the sheriff in private."

Seth removed his hat and set it on the credenza in the streamlined office. Tyler had gotten rid of the massive desk, a number of tables and the overstuffed chairs the former mayor favored.

"Please sit down, Seth. Now that we're alone there's no need to be formal." He sat on an armchair, while Tyler sat opposite him. "When Roger called last night and told me he was going to be out for a while and wanted you to step in and run the sheriff's department until his return, I asked him about Andy Thomas. He told me because of your prior experience as military police and your degree in criminal justice that you were better prepared for the position." Tyler tented his fingers. "And I agree. I had a conference telephone poll with the members of the town council and they were split right down the middle. Three for you and three for Andy, and it was up to me to break the tie."

Seth inclined his head. "Thank you."

Tyler shook his head. "There's no need to thank me, Seth. And I agree with Roger. You're a better pick than Andy, even if he has more seniority. Some folks felt the same way once I challenged Billy Stephens for mayor. They were saying I was too young and inexperienced, that the town was running just fine with Billy. But, it's not about what's just fine. We can't keep losing residents, especially our young people. If they don't leave because they can't find work, then they're dying from drugs. I need you to come up with a proposal from your department as to how we can deal with this opioid problem and after we firm it up I'll present it to the council for their review along with several others for a final vote."

Seth nodded. He hadn't been sworn in five minutes and he had been given his marching orders and knew he had to hit the ground running to give Tyler what he wanted. With Roger out on medical leave, once again the department was down a deputy, and as sheriff, Seth was strictly an administrator exempt from going out on patrols.

"Have you contacted Andy and Connor about my temporary position?" he asked the mayor.

"Yes. Both were sent emails from my office earlier this morning."

"I also have concerns about us being short-staffed. Andy and Connor will be forced to work overtime." Tyler massaged his forehead as he appeared in thought. "I'd like to suggest something," Seth continued.

Tyler met his eyes. "What is it?"

"Contact the mayor over at Mineral Springs and ask if he's willing to lend a couple of their deputies." Mineral Springs and Wickham Falls were two of four towns that made up Johnson County. The neighboring town had a higher population than The Falls and a larger police force.

Tyler stood. "Let me call their mayor and see if he's willing to free up a few of his deputies for a few weeks."

Seth stared at the toes of his spit-shined boots as he waited for Tyler to complete his phone call. His respect for the newly elected mayor went up appreciably; unlike his predecessor, he wasn't in denial when it came to acknowledging that The Falls had an opioid problem.

Tyler ended the call. "Glenn said he can give us two, but we'll have to pay their salaries and benefits. I'll contact the treasurer and find out if they can be paid from one of the discretionary budgets."

Seth did not want to concern himself with who paid them as long as the department had coverage. "Give me a couple of weeks to put together a proposal to address the drug problem and then I'll contact you for a meeting to go over the preliminary sticking points."

"Don't worry about an appointment. My door is always open to all department heads. Calls are going out as we speak to every household in our database to inform them you're now acting sheriff. I've also sent a press release to *The Sentinel* to get into this week's edition before it goes out at the end of the week."

Seth rose and shook the mayor's hand. "Thanks for the vote of confidence."

Although the majority of the populous had voted for Tyler, some of the council members were still loyal to the former mayor.

He made his way down a hallway that led to the station house and unlocked the door to another hallway leading to an area where prisoners were held to be transported to another jurisdiction. Andy and Georgina were in the office, talking quietly to each other when he arrived.

He stared at Georgina, and then Andy. "I'm calling a staff meeting. Georgina, please get Connor on the phone and put him on speaker." Seth sat at his desk. He didn't want to claim Roger's office until after the meeting.

"Seth, Connor's on," Georgina announced.

It took Seth fewer than ten minutes to explain their new duties and responsibilities. He informed them they were getting two deputies from Mineral Springs and that meant Andy and Connor would have preference when it came to choosing shifts. He knew by Andy's expression and body language that he wasn't pleased that he'd been passed over to fill in for Roger.

"Andy, I'd like to know if you're willing to supervise the deputies from Mineral Springs."

The short man with a receding hairline had recently grown a beard to compensate for the loss of the hair on his head. "Do I have a choice?"

A sardonic smile crossed Seth's features. "Yes, you do. If you don't want to supervise them, then I can add it to Connor's duties." He must have gotten Andy's attention when he sat straight. Andy may have been lazy but he definitely wasn't stupid. He knew even as acting sheriff Seth had the authority to promote and demote. And a demotion translated into a reduction in pay. "It's your call, Deputy."

"I'll supervise them."

Seth smiled. "Good. Now that we're all on the same page let's make this department a better place for Roger when he gets back."

"Is he coming back?" Georgina asked.

"Of course," Seth replied. "What makes you think he wouldn't?"

She lifted her shoulders. "I don't know. Even though he's going to be all right, I just can't get the image of him hemorrhaging out of my head."

"It's going to take a lot more than a nosebleed to take out our fearless leader."

"You've got that right," Connor said, his voice coming clearly through the speaker.

"When are the deputies from Mineral Springs coming over?" Andy asked.

"I'm waiting for a call from their sheriff. Meanwhile, Andy, you can knock off at two this afternoon. Connor, I need you to take the two to ten today."

"What about the graveyard shift?" Connor questioned.

Seth dreaded having to start his shift at two in the morning, but it couldn't be helped until he reworked the schedule to include the new deputies. "I'll take it, but only for tonight." That meant he would alternate manning the station house with patrols for the next twenty-four hours. In between, he would go home to pick up several more uniforms and underwear to leave in his locker. "Georgina, I'm going to the hospital to see Roger later this afternoon. If there's anything you want me to bring him, then let me know."

"Can he have visitors?" Connor asked.

"Yes," Seth said.

"I'll probably stop by before I begin my shift. I'm going to hang up now and go back to bed. Later, guys."

Andy got up, put on his gun belt and walked out. "He's not a happy camper," Georgina said under her breath.

"He'll get over it," Seth countered.

Georgina stared at him with her jewel-like eyes. "What if he doesn't, Seth?"

"It's not our problem, Georgina. Maybe this is a wake-up call for Andy that he can't shirk his responsibilities and then expect to be rewarded."

Georgina exhaled an audible breath as she nodded. "You're right. Roger has warned him repeatedly about taking off, so instead of firing or demoting him, he's passed over for a position he's coveted since joining the department."

Seth walked into the office he would occupy until Roger returned. At first, he'd second-guessed his boss's decision to have him fill in for him, but after witnessing Andy's response to supervising the deputies from the next town, he realized Roger was more perceptive than he'd given him credit for.

Natalia sat on the bar stool next to Seth editing the medical section of the proposal he had promised to submit to the mayor and subsequently to the town council for their approval to combat the worsening drug problem. They had finished dinner, cleaned up the kitchen and retreated to the basement to work on the strategy. It had taken more than three hours to go line by line through the eleven-page document, adding statistics and deleting whole sections for conciseness.

A week had passed since Seth's appointment as acting sheriff and with additional deputies from Mineral Springs to offset the dearth of personnel, his revised work schedule proved beneficial when he began his workday at eight in the morning and signed out between the hours of four and six in the afternoon, which allowed them to spend more time together.

Seth cooked outdoors on the patio, gauging the meal to give her time to shower and change before sitting down to eat. They hadn't shared a bed since the night Roger had been admitted to the hospital, but that didn't stop them from kissing and touching each other and stopping just short of making love.

Her fingers stilled on the keys and she read her revisions. Seth had proposed those arrested for drug use should not be criminalized but required to go into treatment. Natalia had given the medical language he needed to describe drug addiction and its damaging and destructive effects of dependency on the body, the family, and the community.

"Do you really think the mayor will agree to setting up a boutique court just to oversee drug cases?" she asked him.

"That's what I'm hoping, Natalia. We have two part-time judges and there's no reason why one can't be assigned to handle drug arrests, which will allow him to become familiar with the offenders. The judge will have the power to mandate them to treatment in lieu of jail.

"Meanwhile if he or she is locked up they are unable to provide for their family. Who do you blame, babe? The addict or the criminal justice system?"

Natalia gave him a long, penetrating stare. "You're preaching to the choir, Seth. Addiction is a disease, not a crime. Putting someone in jail doesn't remedy the problem because even when people are in treatment they'll occasionally relapse, so think of the addict who never gets treatment. They will continue using until they OD, which supports your argument that the town will have to find the money to hire drug counselors."

Seth grimaced. "That's a hurdle that's going to take a lot of convincing to bring to fruition. The town's budget is stretched thin as it is, and now that they have to pay the salaries of the deputies from Mineral Springs a few of the council members are going to fight tooth and nail to vote this down."

"I can't believe they're more interested in pinching pennies than combating a drug crisis."

"You don't know the half of it. Some folks believe the mayor is too young and much too radical for their tastes. People fight change because either they're afraid they will lose control or be left behind."

Natalia chewed her lower lip as she pondered how Seth could get the funds to hire at least two drug counselors. "Have you thought about hosting a fundraiser?"

He shook his head. "I can't get personally involved in raising money because I'm a municipal employee, but you can."

"Me!"

"Yes, you, Natalia. You're a doctor and you're the perfect one to speak at the open monthly town council meeting about addiction and how it's destroying lives, families and neighborhoods. The open meetings are held every third Monday. I'm required to attend because I head a department. And once the fund-raiser is listed on the agenda I will ask for time to talk about law enforcement's involvement."

Natalia pondered his suggestion when he asked, "How many overdoses have you treated since you moved here? I take that back. How many overdoses did you treat when you were in Philadelphia?"

"Calm down, Seth. I didn't say I wouldn't do it."

Seth put his arm around her waist. "I'm sorry, darling, but it's just that I'm fired up about this."

"To answer your question about overdoses. So far I haven't seen anyone whom I suspect is using, but I did have a patient who called me a litany of curses because I told him all prescriptions are forwarded electronically to pharmacies. There was no doubt he was looking for a paper script so he could change the prescribed quantity." Natalia saved the edits on a thumb drive and powered down the laptop and rested her head on his shoulder."

"Thanks for your input on this."

Shifting on the stool, Natalia turned and stared at the man with whom she was falling in love. Six weeks ago she never could have imagined meeting and getting involved with a man, but he'd won her over with his patience and generosity. They were making out but hadn't crossed the line to have sex. She looked forward to coming home and sharing dinner with him, and then sitting together in his basement to watch movies, sports or just sit and listen to music. The space that was converted for entertaining and relaxing had become her favorite room in the house.

They'd developed a habit of dimming the recessed lights and reclining together on the sheepskin area rug.

"I'll do it," Natalia said in a hushed voice.

Seth froze. "Do what?"

"I'll make the presentation to the town council."

He blinked slowly. "Really?"

"Yes, really. Now kiss me so we can seal the deal."

One second she was sitting on the stool and the next she found herself in Seth's arms as he covered her mouth with his and siphoned the breath from her lungs. She went pliant in his embrace while luxuriating in his mouth staking his claim. Her hands were as busy as his as she searched under his T-shirt to run her fingers up and down his back, encountering sinew and muscle when she explored his magnificent body.

He tugged at the hem of her shirt and eased it up and over her head in one smooth motion. The sexual tension, simmering below surface, threatened to explode.

His gorgeous face and body occupied her thoughts when she was awake or asleep. Everything about him invaded her dreams and when she woke it was to her traitorous body throbbing for release.

Wrapping her arms around his neck, Natalia pulled Seth's head down and she kissed him with all of the passion she had withheld from every man in her past. Her lips caressed his until they parted, and she swallowed his breath as their tongues met in a slow, heated joining that sent shock waves throughout her body.

Seth's hands slipped down the length of Natalia's back, cupping her hips as he pressed his groin to her body. A turbulent rising desire held him in a stranglehold that rendered him slightly light-headed. He had to stop kissing her, put some distance between them or embarrass himself when he spilled his passion like a bumbling adolescent in his first sexual encounter. His hands came up and he cradled her face between his palms, breaking off the kiss. Bending slightly, he picked her up, took the stairs to the first story and then the second where he took long strides down the hallway.

Seth carried Natalia into his bedroom and placed her on the bed, his body following hers down. The glow from the dimmed bedside table lamp provided the only source of illumination as he tried to make out her expression.

Would he be able to satisfy her? Would making love with her be different from the other women? The questions kept coming, bombarding Seth relentlessly. Why did it matter so much with Natalia? But he knew the answer before the questions had flooded his mind.

It mattered because she was different, and he had fallen in love with her. He loved her enough to offer his protection, and he loved her enough to want to plan a future with her. He took her face in his hands again. "There's something you need to know before we take this further." Seth registered her intake of breath.

"What is it?"

There came a beat, the sound of their heavy, measured breathing shattering the fragile silence. "I love you."

Chapter Eleven

The emotion in Seth's soft drawling voice triggered a rush of tears Natalia was helpless to hold in check. The tears overflowed, trickled down her cheeks and landed on Seth's hands when he covered her breasts over her bra. Slowly he removed the lacy garment. She bit down on her lip as his fingers traced the outline of one breast, and then the other. A rush of heat and moisture bathed her core. She pressed her knees together as the throbbing increased.

Natalia let out a soulful moan when Seth's mouth replaced his hands. He suckled her at the same time he slid a hand under the drawstring waistband on the cotton lounging pants and caressed her mound. Her head thrashed back and forth. Seth was making her feel things she either had never experienced, or if she did—forgotten. Love and lust merged in a tumultuous passion that made it impossible for her not to move her hips.

Seth pulled a nipple into his mouth, nipping it gently, before giving the other equal attention. He had managed to temper his desire for Natalia because he wanted to offer a passion that would make her forget every man she had known. Forget them because he wanted to become the last man in her life.

"Oh, no!" she gasped.

His head popped up. "What's the matter, baby?" His query was filled with concern.

"Do it, Seth," she pleaded. "Please."

Seth removed her pants and panties, and then undressed himself. He couldn't see, but felt Natalia's eyes following him as he removed a condom from the drawer of the bedside table, and with steady hands he ripped open the packet and slipped the latex sheath over his erection. Natalia's sensual feminine perfume wafted to his nostrils as he moved over her. He spread her legs with his knee and positioned himself at her entrance.

He buried his face between her neck and shoulder, and breathed a kiss on the fragrant skin. "Stop me if I hurt you."

"Don't talk, Seth. Just do it."

"Yes, ma'am," he whispered in her ear.

Natalia closed her eyes and exhaled a slow, audible moan of pleasure when Seth slowly eased his sex inside her. A shared sigh echoed in the room once he was fully sheathed, their bodies fused in a joining that made them one. Her lips quivered as passions cut a swathe up and down her body. His slow, gentle lovemaking swept away doubts and she gave into the passion holding her captive. The fire at the top of her thighs flared even hotter with Seth's quickened thrusts that awakened a response so deep their coming together became an act of complete possession. They lay together, limbs entwined as the seconds ticked into minutes. Seth kissed her forehead.

"Don't move. I have to throw away the condom."

A hint of a smile parted Natalia's lips as she turned over on her belly and closed her eyes. Never had she experienced such an incredible sense of fulfillment. Seth returned, slipped into bed beside her and rested an arm over her hips. The last thing she remembered before falling asleep was his admission that he loved her.

Three days later, Natalia handed Mya a large canvas bag filled with half a dozen bottles of wine when she opened the door to her ring, while Seth cradled two cases of beer against his chest. "You said you didn't want us to bring food, so we decided you could always use some liquid refreshment."

Mya pressed her cheek to Natalia's, and then to Seth's. "Thank you. Please come in. Everyone's out back."

Natalia followed Mya into a house with open rooms, high ceilings and columns that matched the porch posts. French doors and windows let in light and offered an unobstructed view of the outdoors. Wide mullions in the off-white kitchen cabinet doors were details repeated in the home's many windows. The tongue-and-groove plank ceiling, off-white walls, cooking island and breakfast nook reflected comfortable family living.

"Your home is beautiful, Mya."

Mya smiled over her shoulder. "Thank you. I grew up in this house and I had it updated after my parents passed away."

Natalia learned that many residents who'd grown up and stayed in their hometown continued to live in the same house where they were raised. Many of the properties were passed down from generation to generation. And those who'd paid off their mortgages were able to update their homes.

Thinking about homes caused a mysterious smile to soften her mouth when she recalled waking up to enjoy slow, tender lovemaking with Seth. After their initial sexual encounter, it was as if they couldn't get enough of each other, and most nights found her sleeping under his roof. Their relationship had none of the angst she had experienced with Daryl and it was as if Natalia was waiting for something to happen to shatter the happiness that had evaded her. He was out of the house before her and home most nights before her. They weren't able to firm up plans to go fishing or hiking because he now had more administrative responsibility as the head of the sheriff's department. Roger had put in and was approved for an eight-week medical leave, which meant Seth had to attend weekly departmental meetings. He had submitted his proposal to the mayor who said he wouldn't be able to present it to the council members until after Labor Day. The council members had voted unanimously two years ago to cancel the June, July and August meetings because of low turnout.

Mya opened the French doors leading to the patio and outdoor kitchen and garden. "I'm glad it stopped raining and it's not so cool because then we would have to eat indoors."

The patients who came into the clinic complained to Natalia about not seeing the sun for days and with the relentless rain their children were forced to stay inside much to the chagrin of their parents. "The weather is really nice today." The sun was shining and the afternoon temperatures were in the mid-seventies. She'd selected a pale blue slip dress ending at her knees with wide bands that crisscrossed her bare back.

"Look who's here," Mya called when they stepped out onto an expansive patio with an outdoor kitchen.

Giles stood up and came over to greet them. "Let me take those from you," he said to Seth. "Damn, dude, these are heavy." Mya cut her eyes at her husband. "Sorry about that. The D-word just slipped out."

Mya set the bag down on the flagstone floor next to a built-in refrigerator. "Giles, can you please put the wine in the fridge while I introduce Natalia and Seth to everyone."

Natalia smiled and offered the obligatory greeting when Mya acquainted her with her husband's cousins. There was something in Jordan Wainwright's bearing that reminded her of the preppy boys who'd attended college with her. He was tall, dark and handsome with cropped black hair and large hazel eyes that appeared even lighter in his deeply tanned face.

Noah Wainwright shared Jordan's and Giles's height, but that's where the resemblance ended. His shaggy ash-blond hair looked as if he'd styled it with his fingers rather than a comb. Natalia felt as if someone had dropped an ice cube down her back when he stared boldly at her with a pair of blue eyes that seemingly lacked warmth until he smiled. A slender African American woman, carrying a baby boy, came out of the house with Lily who ran over to wrap her arms around Mya's leg. "Natalia, Seth, this beautiful lady is Aziza, Jordan's wife, and the precious cargo she's holding is their son, Maxwell."

"Oh my," Natalia whispered. "He's beautiful." The little boy had inherited his father's swarthy complexion and his mother features. Dark curly hair covered a perfectly rounded little head.

Aziza smiled. "Would you like to hold him? And don't worry—I just changed him."

Natalia took the baby from his mother and cradled him.

She stared into the chubby face with the same eyes as his father's. "You are so handsome, Maxwell," she crooned. "How old are you, Maxwell? Looking at you I'd say you're about six or seven months."

"He's seven months. How did you know?" Aziza asked.

"She's a doctor," Mya said, as she attempted to pry Lily's arms from around her leg. "And her boyfriend is the town's sheriff."

Giles walked over and handed Seth a bottle of beer. "And I've heard he's whipped the sheriff's department into shape since taking over. Natalia, can I get you something to drink?"

"I'm going to wait before I have a beer."

Aziza tightened the elastic band holding her shoulder-length ponytail in place. "I need something a little stronger than a beer now that I'm not breastfeeding."

"How about wine?" Giles asked Aziza.

"Wine's good. Once he got those two little teeth and he began biting me, I knew it was time to stop."

"Does he take the bottle?" Natalia asked.

Aziza nodded. "I alternated giving him a bottle so he wouldn't be that dependent on the breast. By the way, do you and Seth have kids?"

"No. We just started seeing each other."

Aziza stared at Seth as he laughed at something Jordan said. "Now that's one fine brother."

Natalia couldn't stop the heat suffusing her face. "He is okay."

Bending slightly, Mya picked up Lily. "Stop playing yourself, Natalia. You know your man is fine and so do more than half the female population in The Falls."

"Okay. He's fine."

"Speaking of fine brothers, Aziza's brother Alexander Fleming is a ten."

Natalia gave Aziza an incredulous stare. "Your brother is Alex Fleming, the football player?"

Aziza nodded. "Yes. He keeps saying this is his last year, but he just signed another one-year contract. Brandt Wainwright has been bugging him to quit and together they can set up a sports camp for kids whose parents can't afford to send their kids to a sleepaway camp."

With wide eyes, Natalia said, "These are those Wainwrights?" Somehow she hadn't linked Giles with the New York real estate family when Mya said he traveled to New York and the Bahamas for business.

"In living color," Aziza said jokingly.

Natalia wondered how many other people in The Falls realized that a multimillionaire lived among them. Although she wasn't prone to gossip, she had overheard the clinic staff mention Sawyer Middleton's name when they mentioned he'd left Wickham Falls to join the military and returned years later a very wealthy man.

She wondered if it had been a culture shock for Giles to move from what probably was a luxury Manhattan high-rise to a modest two-story farmhouse in rural West Virginia. Wainwright and Middleton. Now she had two more names to add to Seth's list of possible donors for the drug counseling treatment center.

She claimed a seat, still holding Maxwell who'd fallen asleep with his head resting against her breasts. Inhaling the scent associated with babies, she closed her eyes and savored the warmth of the tiny body on hers. She and Daryl had briefly talked about whether they would have children, and she suspected he was conflicted as to whether he wanted to become a father. Becoming a father meant it would take some of her attention off him and Daryl's ego was too fragile if she ignored him for any appreciable amount of time.

Jordan came over and held out his hands. "I'll take him and put him to bed. Zee reads me the riot act if I hold him when he's sleeping."

Reluctantly, she handed the baby to his father. When she glanced up she discovered Seth staring at her with a strange look on his face, and she wondered if he was thinking about the child his wife had that he hadn't been able to claim.

Once Jordan returned Mya announced it was time to eat. She'd set a table with napkins, plates, flatware, wineglasses and water goblets. The men were recruited to carry platters of gilled ribs, chicken, cornon-the-cob, mac and cheese and baked beans to the table. Giles uncorked bottles of red, white and rosé, while Noah had filled several pitchers with beer from a keg. Mya put Lily in a high chair at one end of the rectangular table.

Platters were passed around and all conversation ceased as everyone concentrated on eating. Giles sheepishly admitted that Mya had prepared everything and he'd been recruited to make certain the meat didn't burn. Natalia wanted to tell him he needed Seth to teach him how to cook.

The sun had moved lower and the trees surrounding the property shaded the patio with lengthening shadows as Seth folded his body down onto a chair and stretched out his legs. He definitely had eaten too much. All of the food had been put away and the women had retreated inside, while he, Giles, Jordan and Noah were content to talk about everything from politics to sports.

It was the first full day off he'd had since stepping into the position as acting sheriff. He'd given Andy more responsibility with the hope the man would step up but to no avail. The deputies from Mineral Springs had come to him complaining that Andy tended to be condescending when supervising them, and Seth knew he had to talk to the man or he'd lose the deputies.

His cell phone vibrated and he retrieved it from the pocket of his walking shorts. "What's up, Connor?"

"You told us to let you know about all drug incidents. And we just got a call about a drug situation at the Gainers over on Tanner Road."

He shot up. "What's the situation?"

"The grandmother said one of her grandkids got a hold of something and he's having problems breathing."

"Call the EMTs. I'm on my way." He ended the call. "I'm sorry, I have an emergency and I have to leave." Seth raced inside the house and found Natalia sitting in the living room with Aziza and Mya. "I'm leaving."

She stood. "What's wrong?"

"There's a possible OD."

Natalia reached for her tote. "I'm coming with you. I always carry naloxone with me."

Seth took her hand and together they raced across the road and got into the Charger. He floored the gas and within seconds the speedometer exceeded sixty miles per hour. He came to a screeching halt and was out of the car and running up the porch when the door opened.

An elderly woman was crying and wringing her hands. "He got a hold of something and he's real sick."

"Where is he?"

"He's in the back bedroom."

Seth found the teenage boy on the bed gasping for breath. Natalia entered the room and sat on the side of the bed. She held the boy's head and sprayed a solution into his nostrils. The antidote took effect immediately. He opened his eyes and screamed for his mother.

Natalia looked at Seth. "He's going to be all right." The words were barely off her tongue when the medical technicians walked into the room.

"Dr. Hawkins took care of him."

"Good work, Doc."

Seth waited for them to leave to confront the child's grandmother. "Mrs. Gainer, where did your grandson get the drugs?"

The elderly woman looked at him as if he were speaking a foreign language. "I don't know what you're talking about. Ain't no drugs in the house except my arthritis medicine."

Natalia joined them in the living room. "You're not telling the truth. The solution I sprayed into your grandson's nose reverses the effects of an opioid overdose. He had trouble breathing and his heartbeat was slowing and the next phase was a coma and death. If the drugs aren't in the house, then he had to have gotten them from somewhere. Either he gets help or the next time you'll be planning his funeral."

Mrs. Gainer ran trembling hands over her wiry gray hair held in place with a hairnet. "I swear I don't know where he got his pills. I can't do nothing with him. All he does is sleep and when he wakes up, he goes out and comes home to sleep some more. He's only fourteen and he won't listen to me, his momma or his stepfather. I keep telling them the boy is hopeless."

"Willie isn't hopeless, Mrs. Gainer," Seth said. "The boy is addicted to drugs. I'm not going to talk to him tonight because I want him clearheaded when I come back tomorrow. Tell him he better be here because I want to know where he's getting his drugs. And if he runs and I find him, then he's going to be locked up."

She nodded like a bobblehead doll. "I'll tell him."

Seth reached for Natalia's hand and led her out of

the house. "Somebody is selling drugs in The Falls and I won't rest until I find them."

"How are you going to do that?"

"I'm going to have a long talk with Willie and hopefully he'll give up his dealer." He gave her fingers a gentle squeeze. "Let's go home."

"I can't believe you worked so hard on the proposal for the mayor to approve it, and he has to wait until September to present it."

"Three months will go by quickly. What I can't believe is that I finally get one whole day off and I still have to answer a call."

"Are you going in tomorrow?"

"Probably, but only for a few hours after I talk to Willie." Seth waited for Natalia to get into the car, and then came around to sit beside her. He stared at her delicate profile. "Are you sorry you got involved with me?"

Her head came around. "Why would you ask me that?"

"Because I can't spend as much time with you as you'd like. That it would've been better if you'd hooked up with a nine-to-five, weekends-off guy."

A slight frown appeared between her eyes. "Stop it, Seth. Now that you're acting sheriff, I get to see you a lot more than I did before. And don't forget, if I worked at a hospital, we'd get to see each other even less. I'm also not working a nine-to-five with weekends off schedule, either. I don't have a problem with our arrangement, and I don't want or need a man in my face twenty-four seven. Think of the time we spend together as quality time."

Leaning to his right, Seth angled his head and kissed her. "Thanks for the pep talk."

Seth tapped the Start engine button and executed a smooth U-turn. He did not want a rerun of his life where he had left a woman he loved for months and she sought out another man to assuage her loneliness. He had tried to keep regular hours but knew that wasn't going to continue to be possible. He knew he would have to resolve the problem with Andy, but first he had to talk to Roger.

Seth sat on a rocker on Roger's porch staring out at the wildflowers his wife grew in large clay pots. "I'm going to give him a verbal warning and if he doesn't change, then I'm going to write him up. After that, I'm going to lower the hammer and fire him."

Roger rested his hands on his shrinking belly. "There was a time when I would've gotten rid of Andy because I wouldn't tolerate anyone not doing their job. But I'm tired, Seth. Twenty years in Uncle Sam's army and another twenty policing Wickham Falls has taken its toll on me. I was talking to my wife the other day and she wants me to give it up. If I collect social security, my military pension and the one from the town, we can live quite comfortably. The house is paid off, all the kids are gone and don't ask for anything, so I'm going to put in my papers."

"Are you serious, Roger?"

"Serious as a heart attack. I suppose I shouldn't say that when I came so close to checking out. I'm going to call the mayor and tell him I'm out and that you should stay on as sheriff. That will give you the authority you need to deal with Andy. My four-year term is up in March, which means you'll have to campaign for the position."

"That's not something I'm looking forward to. I don't like cheesing and slapping backs for votes."

"All you have to do is smile at the ladies and kiss their babies and you're a shoo-in."

"Yeah, right. Something tells me Andy will decide to run against me."

"If he does, then he's going to lose—big-time."

"Maybe I won't fire him before I announce that I'm running for the office. The dynamics in the station house should be very interesting."

Roger chuckled. "Oh, to be a fly on the wall."

"Knowing how much Georgina dislikes him, she'll probably videotape it."

The older man sobered. "I think the best thing to happen to me was having the medical episode because I still would've continued to eat all the wrong food and definitely not exercise. Every morning I get up and walk down to the church and then walk back. I clocked it as a mile. Once I lose my first twenty pounds, I'm going for two miles a day."

"You can come over and use my treadmill when the weather's bad."

"No, Seth. I'm not going to intrude on you and Dr. Hawkins. Don't look at me like that. It's all over town that you and that pretty lady doctor are as thick as thieves."

"Well, damn," Seth said under his breath.

"No good, son. It's about time you settled down and made some babies. There's no doubt they're going to be beautiful. When my wife saw her for the first time, she thought she was the television journalist Tamron Hall."

It wasn't the first time a man talked about Natalia's beauty. With or without makeup, she was stunning. "I'm a lucky man."

"Make certain you don't forget that or you'll lose her. Dudes are lining up waiting for you to break up with her."

A shiver of annoyance gripped Seth. He had no intention of breaking up with Natalia. He'd confessed to being in love with her, but she had yet to verbalize her feelings for him. Even in the throes of passion she did not blurt out that four-letter word he wanted and needed from her. Seth knew he couldn't put pressure on Natalia and risk losing her.

"Keep up the good work with your diet and exercise. I'll call before I drop by again."

Seth drove back to the house expecting to see Natalia. She wasn't there but he knew she couldn't have gone far because her SUV was parked in her driveway. He'd given her a set of keys to the house along with the code to disarm the security system. His talk with Willie Gainer was fraught with frustration because the kid refused to reveal where he'd gotten the pills, and he suspected the teenager was too frightened to snitch on his dealer.

He was in the kitchen reading the local paper when he heard the front door open. "I'm in the kitchen," he called out.

Natalia walked into the kitchen and brushed a kiss over his mouth. "Hey, coffee breath," she teased.

"Do you want me to brew you a cup?"

"No, thanks." She set her tote on the floor. "I was across the road hanging out with Mya."

"It's nice that you've become friends."

"I really like her and Lily."

Seth met her eyes. "You like babies."

Natalia climbed up on the stool next to him. "Yep."

"You want children."

"Are you asking me if I want children?" He nodded. "Then the answer is yes, but only if I'm married."

His eyebrows lifted. "You have to *be* married?"

"Yes. Why does that surprise you?"

"I just thought you were one of those modern liberated women—"

"I am liberated," she interrupted, "but there are some requisites I try to stick to. And that is I want to be married when I have my children."

Seth turned his head so she could see his smile. Natalia insisting on marriage before motherhood was something he also wanted and believed in. "You seem to be getting in a lot of practice with Lily."

"I like her because she's feisty. When she grows up I doubt if she's going to let anyone take advantage of her."

"She's a Wainwright, Natalia, and that means she was born into a prominent New York family with immense wealth and influence."

"The same could be said for Aziza's son, Maxwell. I can't believe he's so chill. Most babies his age are fussy, but he's different. When he's awake he just looks around taking in everything."

"Children, like grown folks, have different personalities."

"How was your meeting with Willie?"

"It went nowhere. The kid's scared and I decided not to push him. I stopped to see Roger and he told me he's resigning."

A beat passed. "Does this mean you'll be the sheriff?"

"Yes. Roger's term ends next March, which means I have nine months to campaign for the position."

"Are you?"

"Yes. I won't have to do much electioneering. Lawn signs and a few buttons are the norm."

Natalia put her arms around his neck, pulling his head down. "Congratulations. I have to register with the board of elections so I can vote for you."

Seth kissed her, increasing the pressure until her lips parted under his. The moans coming from her throat were his undoing when he swept her up and carried her effortlessly out of the kitchen and up the staircase to the bedroom. It had been a week since they'd last made love and he likened it to a drought. Now he was given the chance to assuage his thirst and he planned to let his body talk for him. He loved her. Wanted to marry her. And he wanted her to have their children.

Mouths joined, they undressed each other as articles of clothing lay strewn over the floor. They came together like runaway freight trains speeding on the same track toward a head-on collision. Natalia was totally uninhibited and shocked him when her mouth charted a sensual exploration from his mouth to the soles of his feet before reversing direction. Seth feared losing control, that she had the power to control him in and out of bed. Anchoring his hands under her armpits, he eased her up, flipped her over on her back and entered her in one strong thrust.

Fires hotter than any other he'd known threatened to incinerate Seth, and he knew he had to release his damped-down passions before passing out. *Marry me, marry me, marry me.* The silent litany played over and over in his mind until he had to clamp his teeth together to keep from blurting out what lay in his heart. They soared to heights of shared ecstasy and then floated back to reality to succumb to a sated sleep for lovers.

Chapter Twelve

For the second time in two months, the mayor issued a press release informing the residents that Sheriff Roger Jensen tendered his resignation and Seth Collier would replace him and serve out his term. He was sworn in again, and this time he invited Natalia to attend the swearing-in ceremony.

Now that he was officially the sheriff of Wickham Falls, Seth had a long, in-depth conversation with Andy about his attitude, his inability to supervise those under him and said it would be the last time he would speak to him about his conduct. He informed him that his next reprimand would be in writing, and the final dismissal. He told Andy they had to work as a united team to combat the town's drug problem because he could not do it alone and that he was going to recommend he attend a conference in the state capital addressing the opioid crisis. Andy appeared remorseful and thanked Seth for giving him another chance.

Mother Nature had conspired to punish the region with torrential rain and two F-1 tornadoes; the first forced the mayor and the Chamber of Commerce to cancel the Fourth of July three-day celebration, and the second was in mid-August. Mineral Springs sustained greater property damage than Wickham Falls and volunteers were dispatched to assist the neighboring town.

Seth returned home late one night to find Natalia on the porch waiting for him. Leaning over, he kissed her. "What are you doing up so late?"

"I wanted to show you this." She handed him her cell phone.

Seth read the text message from her ex, and her response. He had asked for her address because he wanted to return Oreo. "Why show me this when you've already sent him your address?"

"We're practically living together so I don't want him to show up and then I'd have to explain why he's here."

Seth kissed her again. "Don't worry, babe. I promise to behave."

She smiled. "You better behave. Daryl would love a confrontation so he can sue you."

"When is he coming?"

"Tomorrow."

"Why tomorrow, Natalia?"

"He said he's going on vacation and doesn't want to board Oreo. I called Henry to ask him for the day off."

"I'm scheduled to work tomorrow but I'll take off in case you need backup."

"I don't think I'm going to need backup," she said.

"I'm still taking off."

"I'm going upstairs to shower and get ready for bed. Are you coming?"

"Not yet. It's the first time in days it hasn't rained, and I want to do a little stargazing."

He ruffled her hair. "Don't stay up too late," Natalia said.

"I won't."

Natalia came down off the porch when a shiny black town car pulled up in front of her rental. Her heart rate increased when the driver got out and opened the rear door. She held her breath when the man she never believed she would see again stepped out and walked toward her.

She ignored the cut of his light gray suit, imported leather slip-ons, silk tie and custom-made shirt with monogrammed cuffs. He was thinner and his hair grayer than she'd remembered. Daryl Owens wasn't as handsome as he was attractive. Fastidious almost to a fault, he had standing appointments for haircuts and facials, and his dark brown complexion radiated good health.

Natalia folded her hands at her waist. "Where's Oreo?"

Daryl placed a foot on the first step and angled his head. "You look good, baby."

Her eyelids fluttered wildly. "I'm not your baby. I asked you where my dog is."

"He's with a friend."

Natalia struggled not to lose her temper. "Liar! You told me you were bringing Oreo."

"I said that because I knew you wouldn't see me otherwise."

"You've got that right! I wouldn't have, and I never want to see you again!" Natalia was screaming at the top of her lungs and she didn't care who saw her or heard her.

Daryl mounted the steps and held her upper arms in a firm grip. "Calm down, Natty. I know you're upset about Oreo but please let me explain."

"There's nothing you can say that I need to hear. Now take your hands off me."

"I will, but hear me out first."

"You heard the lady. Take your hands off her."

Natalia and Daryl turned, as if they'd choreographed the move beforehand, to see Seth coming toward them. She had been so engrossed in arguing with Daryl that she wasn't aware Seth had come out of his house.

Daryl glared at him. "Who's asking?"

Seth stalked Daryl like a large cat. "I'm not going to tell you again to take your hands off her."

His fingers loosened slightly. "And if I don't?"

"Don't start with him, Daryl," Natalia pleaded softly.

The dapper lawyer narrowed his eyes. "Why? Is he going to beat me up?"

"I'm not going to give you what you need for causing my fiancée so much pain, which is a good thumping. As the sheriff of Wickham Falls, I'm going to arrest your fancy ass and after you spend the night in our lockup, you can plead your case to our judge. I want to caution you that folks around here don't take kindly to you assaulting their doctor."

Daryl dropped his hands as if her arms suddenly had become heated metal. "You're her fiancé?"

Seth cupped his ear. "I don't hear an echo. You heard right the first time."

Daryl snorted. "If she's your fiancée, why isn't she wearing a ring?"

Seth approached Daryl and towered over him. "She told me about you taking off with her ring and the dog. And because I didn't want her to relive that trauma I plan to give her an engagement ring the day before we're to be married." A sardonic smile twisted his mouth. "Your driver is waiting, and make certain he doesn't speed on the way out of town because we impound the cars of speeders."

"Have a nice life," Daryl spat out.

Seth put up two fingers. "Deuces, clown."

Natalia's knees were shaking so hard she doubted whether they would support her and sank down to the top step. She did not want to believe the audacity of her ex coming from Philly under the pretense he wanted to return her pet when he actually wanted a reconciliation. And Seth compounded it with a lie that they were engaged, and there was no doubt Daryl would return home and spread the rumor that she was engaged to be married to a lawman in a town that barely made the map. She spoke to her mother two or three times a month and at no time had she mentioned she was involved with a man.

As the car slowly maneuvered away from the curb, she watched the taillights until it disappeared from her line of vision. Natalia shrank when Seth folded his tall frame down next to her. "Why did you lie to him?" The question was flat, emotionless.

"I had to say something to get him to leave and take what I told him as sheriff to never come back"

"I don't need you to fight my battles."

"You think not? He continued to manhandle you even after you told him to take his hands off you."

"You didn't have to tell him we were getting married. You did to me what I'd allowed Daryl to do to me. And that is to make decisions for me because he thought he knew what was best. And knowing him, he's going back to Philly and telling everyone he knows that I'm engaged. Then my family is going to blow up my phone with questions that I can't or won't answer."

Seth stood and glared down at Natalia. He was in an emotional tumult because he had allowed Natalia to break through the wall where he had kept women at a distance since his divorce. Not only had he fallen in love with her, but he also wanted her in his life— for all time. When he'd told her ex that they were engaged, he wanted it to be true.

"You're going to have to make up your mind, Natalia. Either we're in this together or we can go back to being neighbors."

"You don't get it, do you?" Natalia asked.

"Get what?"

"We've never talked about marriage. In fact, neither of us has ever mentioned it."

"That's because you've never given me an opening."

She gave him a wide-eyed stare. "Oh, now you're blaming me." Natalia shook her head. "No, Seth. This is not on me. You talk about how I'm your fiancée, and then expect me to go along with it. I'm not one of your deputies or men under your command in the Marines where you give orders and expect them to be followed without question. I wasted too many years with a man who deemed it was his right to bend me to his will, and I'll be damned if I'm going to have a rerun with you." Turning on her heel Natalia walked into her house, leaving Seth to stare at the space where she had been.

"Why do you look as if you've lost your best friend?"

Natalia closed her eyes and struggled to keep her emotions in check. It had been more than three weeks since the two men she'd known intimately had walked out of her life. "I have."

Mya moved over to sit next to her on the love seat. "Seth?"

"Yes."

"Talk to me."

Natalia she told Mya everything about her relationship with Daryl and how she was given a second chance at love when she met Seth and then about his confrontation with Daryl. "He didn't have to tell Daryl we were engaged to be married when it's the farthest thing from the truth."

"You think not, Natalia?"

"It's a lie."

"It's not a lie," Mya insisted. "He's in love with you and he does want to marry you."

"That's not the point. The problem is he never asked me what I want, just like Daryl never did. I don't intend to share my life or my future with a man who believes he knows what's best for me."

"But he does want to marry you," Mya insisted.

"How do you know this?"

"Seth stopped by the house one night and I overheard him talking to Giles about how much he loves you and that he's finally found the woman he wants to spend the rest of his life with and she just happens to be his neighbor." Natalia clapped a hand over her mouth. "Has he told you that he loves you?" Mya asked.

"Yes. Once when we were making love and men will say anything in the throes of passion."

"What about you? Have you told him you love him?"

"No."

"Why not, Natalia?"

"I didn't want to ruin what we have. No, *had*. Every time I tell a man that I love him, he takes it as a signal to crap all over me."

"Why are you lumping Seth into the same category as those other losers?"

"Thrice burned, thrice shy."

"That's a lot of bologna and you know it. Sometimes, we have to kiss a few frogs before we find our prince. Believe me, I've kissed more than my share of frogs before I realized Giles was a keeper. Last month we began trying for a baby and hopefully by this time next year we'll give Lily a brother or a sister." Mya reached for Natalia's hand. "Now I want you to promise me that you're going to give Seth a chance to come to his senses before you write him off completely."

"Why is it that I'm so secure as a doctor, but I'm a mess when it comes to dealing with a man?"

"Do you think it's easy for a man?"

"No, but I don't think I'm being difficult. Asking him to consult me before planning our future is a perfectly reasonable request."

"I don't think you're difficult, Natalia. Just promise me you'll not write Seth off until the two of you are able to work things out."

"It's already been three weeks."

Mya smiled. "Give him another week, and if he doesn't come around, then you'll know it's over. But if you do get back together, then I'd like you to consider having me as your matron of honor."

Natalia eased her hand from Mya's. "If things work out and I marry Seth, you will be my matron of honor."

Natalia pressed her cheek to Mya's. "Thanks for hearing me out."

"That's what sisters are for."

She left Mya's house and scanned the road for oncoming cars and then dashed across. Natalia didn't know if Seth was at home because no light shone through the windows and his pickup was parked in the driveway adjacent to hers. He garaged the Charger, so she didn't know if he had taken it out.

She felt better now that she had talked to Mya. And as promised, she would give Seth another week before relegating him to her past as she had with the other men in her life.

After walking up the steps to the porch, she went completely still. A dark figure rose from the chair and she detected the familiar scent of Seth's cologne. There was enough illumination from the light over the door to see his expression. Their three-week separation had taken its toll. His face was thinner, and there were new lines bracketing his strong mouth. "We need to talk."

She nodded. "Yes, we do."

"May I come in?"

Natalia unlocked the door and held it open. "Yes. We'll talk in the living room." Natalia sat on the edge of the love seat staring directly at Seth who'd folded his body down to an armchair. She missed him so much that she felt like weeping. It wasn't only his lovemaking, but the way he always made her feel protected whenever they were together. And she missed that they were so cognizant of the other's moods. She knew when he'd had a rough day at work or felt his frustration in trying to identify who was supplying the drugs that were slowly destroying lives.

Seth curbed the urge to cross the room and sit beside Natalia. A sad smile twisted his mouth. "Do you know how long it's been since we've last been together?"

Natalia blinked slowly. "No."

"Three weeks, four days and approximately fourteen hours."

She laughed softly. "What about the minutes and seconds?"

"I lost track of those."

Natalia quickly sobered. "What do you want to talk about?"

Seth sandwiched his hands between his knees. "I want to apologize for being presumptuous. For assuming because we were sleeping together that if I proposed marriage you would accept it without question."

"You still don't get it, do you? You've never proposed, Seth. How can I accept or reject your proposal if you don't ask?"

His hands tightened into fists. "What do you want me to do?"

Natalia gave him a long, penetrating stare.

"For an intelligent man, you can be really obtuse. Ask me properly, Seth."

"Ask you what?" he asked.

"I need to hear you propose to me."

Seth didn't want to believe he had wasted three weeks pining for Natalia when all he had to do was open his mouth and ask her to become his wife. He had told her he loved her, but it was apparent that wasn't enough. "Natalia Rachel Hawkins, will you do me the honor of becoming my wife and hopefully the mother of our children?"

"Hey, how do you know my middle name?"

"I'll tell you after you give me your answer."

"Yes, Seth Collier, I will marry you and have your babies."

Seth moved over and sat next to Natalia and placed tiny kisses all over her face. "I ran your license plate through our database with a protected server and found out everything I needed to know about my beautiful, sexy neighbor."

She giggled. "That's snooping."

"No, it's not. I had to find out what I was in for once I decided I was going to snap you up before the other guys in The Falls hit on you."

"That wasn't going to happen because you had me when you offered to help me paint Chandler's kitchen. I knew then that you were a keeper."

Seth kissed her forehead. "I promise never to make a decision for us without running it past you first."

Natalia pressed her mouth to his. "I'm going to hold you to that promise."

"Do you want an engagement ring now or at the rehearsal dinner?"

"I'd like one to celebrate our first anniversary."

Euphoria swept over Seth and he felt slightly light-headed. He had waited for Natalia to come to him day after day, night after night, while stubbornness and false masculine pride kept him from approaching her. Then he knew if he didn't take the initiative and apologize for doing to her what her ex had done, he would lose her forever.

"What about dates? We have to decide on one before we call our folks with the news?"

"I moved here on Saturday, May 1, so why not the first of May next year?"

"Then May 1 it is."

"I'd like Mya and my sister to be my attendants."

Seth smiled. It was apparent Natalia had already planned their wedding. "I'm going to ask Giles to stand in as my best man and Roger as a groomsman. By that time, he should be svelte enough to fit into a tuxedo without popping the buttons of the vest."

"I love you so much. Kiss me, darling, to seal the deal."

"I remember when you first said that to me, we wound up in bed making love," Seth said, reminding her of when he'd committed himself to her physically and emotionally.

"And it was the first time you told me you loved me."

"And it won't be the last." Seth kissed her and then whispered in her ear what he wanted to do to her.

Natalia giggled in anticipation. "No! That's nasty!"

"Good nasty or bad nasty?"

"I don't know. Let's go the bedroom so I can find out which one I like best."

Epilogue

The weather was perfect for a white wedding. Natalia and Seth had decided to hold the ceremony and reception outdoors under a tent on the church lawn. She had met his family when they came up from Savannah the weekend before, and her parents and siblings had arrived two days before the ceremony.

Wickham Falls had changed in a year. Seth had run unopposed in the election and won by an overwhelming margin. The town council had accepted his proposal to wage a war on drugs and thanks to the generosity of Giles Wainwright and Sawyer Middleton, who'd donated the money, they could rent office space in the building housing the newspaper and an accounting firm, and cover the salaries of a full-time and a part-time substance abuse counselor. Natalia had volunteered her services as medical director and all first responders were required to carry naloxone to reverse the effects of a drug overdose.

Natalia stopped pacing in the small room at the church when she heard a knock on the door. "Come in." Her sister looked like the prototype for an exquisite African American doll in the shrimp-colored gown that accentuated her curvy petite body. "You look so pretty, Rena."

"Never mind me. I'm certain Seth is going to lose it when he sees you."

It had taken Natalia a month before she found a gown she felt comfortable wearing. It was a Monique Lhuillier strapless design with a sweetheart neckline, seeded pearl bodice and a rose-pink sash that flowed down the back of the chiffon skirt to the hemline. On her head she wore a chapel veil attached to a feather headpiece that would be removed following the ceremony.

There was another knock on the door and Dr. Pearce Hawkins entered in his wedding finery. He was still incredibly handsome for a man in his early sixties. Pearce had been a very eligible bachelor until he met Sylvia who hadn't made it easy for him to claim her as his wife. He had asked her out every week for six months before she agreed and because she didn't appear eager for a second date, Pearce proposed marriage to convince her he was serious about her.

Pearce and Seth bonded within minutes of meeting each other. Pearce had openly admitted that he liked Seth a lot better than that pompous cretin she'd first planned to marry.

He offered Natalia his arm and she placed her hand

over the sleeve of his tuxedo jacket. "Let's go and get you married because your young man is wearing a hole in the carpet pacing up and down like a big cat."

Holding up her skirt, Natalia walked down the hallway to a door the led to the entrance of the tent. She bit back a scream when she saw Mya in a rose-pink gown holding her bridal bouquet in one hand and a flower bedecked white basket with a tiny brown poodle puppy with Seth's wedding ring on a pink ribbon tied around its neck.

Mya handed her the bouquet. "Seth says this is his wedding gift to you. Cocoa is your ring bearer. Giles and I will take care of him until you return from your honeymoon."

The wedding planner approached the wedding party. "We're starting now." She signaled for the two men standing at the entrance to the tent to open the flaps. Prerecorded music played softly as Mya proceeded slowly over the white carpet as those in attendance pointed to the puppy in the basket. Serena followed with Roger Jensen who had shed weight and appeared ten years younger.

And when the familiar chords of the "Wedding March" echoed throughout the tent, Natalia looked straight ahead, her eyes meeting her future husband's for the first time in more than twelve hours. Her breath caught in her throat when she stared at his ramrod-straight back, willing him to turn around. Giles did turn to catch a glimpse of her and nudged Seth with his elbow.

It seemed like an eternity before she reached his side and her father placed her hand on Seth's arm, indicating he had relinquished responsibility for his daughter to the man who'd promised to love her forever.

She stared up at him through her lashes unable to believe she could feel this happy. It was Sunday, May 1 and the significance of the date would stay with her forever. Seth's head came down in slow-motion and he barely touched her mouth with his.

"Hold up, Sheriff Collier," the pastor admonished, laughing. "She's not your wife until I complete the ceremony." Those sitting close enough heard the clergyman burst into uncontrollable laughter. The noise woke Cocoa, who let out a piercing sound that elicited more laughter.

Seth nodded. "Let's do it so I can seal this deal."

Natalia lowered her head and eyes. Seal the deal had become a catchphrase for them making love. They planned to spend their wedding night at the house and Giles's wedding gift to them had been to charter a private jet to fly them down to the Bahamas the following morning. He had arranged for them to stay in a private villa at a Wainwright vacation property for a week in what had been touted as a tropical paradise.

Her hand shook slightly when, after repeating their vows, Seth slipped a gold band on her finger. She untied the ribbon around the puppy's neck and slipped a matching band on his hand. When the pastor told Seth he could kiss his wife, he bent slightly, picked her up and met her eyes.

"Are you ready to seal this deal, Mrs. Collier?"

Natalia scrunched up her nose. "You bet, Mr. Collier. Let's do it."

The skirt of her gown flowed over his tuxedo as she put her arms around his neck and kissed him with all the passion she summoned from a place she hadn't known existed.

Thunderous applause filled the tent as camera phones recorded the instant their Wickham Falls sheriff had claimed their lady doctor as his own.

* * * * *

MILLS & BOON

Coming next month

CINDERELLA'S NEW YORK CHRISTMAS
Scarlet Wilson

Leo finished the call. New York. He'd wanted to go back there for days. But somehow he knew when he got there, the chances of getting a flight back to Mont Coeur to spend Christmas with his new family would get slimmer and slimmer.

Here, he'd had the benefit of a little time. Everything in New York was generally about work, even down to the Christmas charity ball he was obligated to attend. As soon as he returned to the States…

His stomach clenched. The Christmas ball. The place he always took a date.

For the first time, the prospect of consulting his little black book suddenly didn't seem so appealing.

'Nearly done.' Anissa smiled as he approached.

'I have to go back to New York.'

Her face fell. 'What?'

She was upset. He hated that. He hated that fleeting look of hurt in her eyes.

'It's business. A particularly tricky deal.'

Anissa pressed her lips tight together and nodded automatically.

The seed of an idea that had partially formed outside burst into full bloom in his head. He hated that flicker of pain he'd seen in her eyes when she'd talked about being in Mont Coeur and being permanently reminded of what she'd lost.

Maybe, just maybe he could change things for her. Put a little sparkle and hope back into her eyes. Something that he ached to feel in his life too.

'Come with me.' The words flew out of his mouth.

Her eyes widened. 'What?'

He nodded, as it all started to make sense in his head. 'You said you've never really had a proper holiday. Come with me. Come and see New York. You'll love it in winter. I can take you sightseeing.'

Anissa's mouth was open. 'But…my job. I have lessons booked. I have chalets to clean.'

He moved closer to her. 'Leave them. See if someone can cover. I have a Christmas ball to attend and I'd love it if you could come with me.' His hands ached to reach for her, but he held himself back. 'I called you Ice Princess before, how do you feel about being Cinderella?'

He could see her hesitation. See her worries.

But her pale blue eyes met his. There was still a little sparkle there. Still a little hope for him.

Her lips turned upwards. 'Okay,' she whispered back as he bent to kiss her.

Continue reading
CINDERELLA'S NEW YORK CHRISTMAS
Scarlet Wilson

Available next month
www.millsandboon.co.uk

COMING SOON!

We really hope you enjoyed reading this book. If you're looking for more romance, be sure to head to the shops when new books are available on

Thursday
4th October

To see which titles are coming soon, please visit
millsandboon.co.uk

LET'S TALK
Romance

For exclusive extracts, competitions
and special offers, find us online:

f facebook.com/millsandboon

⊙ @millsandboonuk

𝕐 @millsandboon

Or get in touch on 0844 844 1351*

For all the latest titles coming soon, visit
millsandboon.co.uk/nextmonth

Want even more
ROMANCE?

Join our bookclub today!

'Mills & Boon books, the perfect way to escape for an hour or so.'

Miss W. Dyer

'Excellent service, promptly delivered and very good subscription choices.'

Miss A. Pearson

'You get fantastic special offers and the chance to get books before they hit the shops'

Mrs V. Hall

**Visit millsandbook.co.uk/Bookclub
and save on brand new books.**

MILLS & BOON